We Got Spirit

by Lara Bergen

SCHOLASTIC INC.

ISBN 978-0-545-56283-6

12 11 10 9 8 7 6 5 4 3 2 1 14 15 16 17 18 19/0

Printed in the U.S.A. 40
First Scholastic printing, January 2014

TWO, FOUR, SIX, EIGHT!
WHO DO WE APPRECIATE?
ANNA BLOOM!!!

CHAPTER 1

"We got spirit!

Yeah! Yeah!

We got spirit!

Yeah! Yeah!

We got what? What? What? What?

A what-what-what-what-what-what-what?

We got SPIRIT!"

"Go, Falcons!"

Sophia lunged forward, lifting one arm straight up and punching the other out sharply to the side.

"Very nice, ladies!" Coach Casey said, nodding. "I could understand every word that time. At the rate you're learning these sideline chants, you're going to be in great shape by game day. Okay!" She clapped. "Water break. Everyone hydrate." She grinned and rubbed her palms together. "Coming up: jump drills!"

Ugh.

Sophia didn't groan out loud, but a few other girls did, including Sadie, another sixth grader, who was smiling — as usual — but panting as well.

"My legs are still sore from *yesterday*," Sadie said, squeezing her suntanned thighs.

Sophia's legs were a little sore, too, but she was used to the feeling by now. In fact, she kind of liked being reminded of how strong her muscles were getting and how much more they could do. After all, as Coach Casey said, "no pain, no gain!" It was definitely true.

Sophia had thought the two-hour clinics leading up to tryouts had been hard, but they were nothing compared to the training camp the girls who'd made the squad had been going to ever since. Four nonstop hours of practice in the school gym each and every afternoon. It had been tough and exhausting. But also so much fun! And now it was almost over, Sophia suddenly realized. *Real* school, with two-hour cheerleading practices after, was starting the very next week. Her heart stalled, then lurched as she thought about it. In just a few days, she'd be a sixth grader at Fairview Middle School.

And a Falcons cheerleader, too.

"Hey, Sophia, is this yours?" A dark-skinned girl with an I ♥ NY T-shirt glided toward her. She had a metal water bottle in each hand. She smiled and held out to Sophia the one that had a big chess king stamped on the side.

"Thanks!" Sophia said as she took it. "*What ever* made you think it was mine?"

"Wow. I don't know," Kendall said, acting bewildered. "Just a lucky guess, I suppose."

They both knew that Sophia was the one and only former elementary school chess champion on the new Fairview Middle School cheer squad. Just months earlier, chess had been the most important thing in Sophia's life next to school, books, and her family. Yet when she got the flyer in the mail about summer cheerleader tryouts, she could almost feel her whole body reset. It was like a switch had been flipped — or a window had been opened, letting a fresh breeze in.

All her life, she'd been the "smart girl." She'd even heard some people call her the Brain. While she liked being smart and was proud of her grades, Sophia couldn't wait to show people, and maybe herself, too, that she was more than a chess-playing straight-A student with a mouthful of braces and the longest hair in school.

The really amazing thing was she'd actually made the twenty-girl squad. Out of *all* the new sixth graders who had tried out for the team, she was one of just six who had been picked. It was nice to know that with cheerleading, just like with chess and school, hard work and practice really paid off in the end. It was also *very* nice to have met Kendall, who'd made the whole experience extra fun.

Kendall was also new to cheering, and she was new to Fairview, too. She'd moved there that summer with her family from New York City, where she'd done gymnastics since she was four years old. Sophia was the first girl Kendall met at tryouts, and they instantly hit it off. Kendall had even taught her how to do a cartwheel — something Sophia had thought she'd never be able to do. Unfortunately, Sophia messed up a little when she did one at tryouts — but she still earned enough points to make the squad. After weeks of more practice, however, she was hitting them perfectly all the time now.

Kendall took a quick sip from her own water bottle. "Hey, want to come home with me?" she asked Sophia. "I got some new clothes for school. You can tell me what you think. What do kids here wear on the first day of school, anyway?"

"Uh . . ." Sophia took a drink, too, and shrugged a little. "Don't ask me." She grinned. "Honestly, I was actually wondering the same thing."

In elementary school, Sophia had been more than happy not to worry too much about clothes. She used to like dresses a lot but stopped wearing them in fourth grade because nobody else seemed to. Since then, she'd stuck to the basics: T-shirts and jeans. Plus, that was really all her mom could afford. If the clothes matched and were clean, she wore them and crossed her fingers that she wouldn't stand out.

But middle school was different. She wasn't just starting a new chapter of her life. She was starting a whole new book. And if chess had taught her anything, it was how important first moves were. Could one careless step, like wearing the wrong thing, lose you the whole match? Sophia wondered.

"I know who we *should* ask," Sophia said, turning toward two girls near the bleachers. One was holding up a little mirror while the other expertly straightened her hair bow. As soon as it was perfect, they traded off the mirror, along with a business-like nod.

M&M. Madison and Mia. Best friends so close — and so popular — that they were better known by a single name. They'd both gone to school with Sophia since kindergarten and were by far the most stylish girls she knew. They were also girls she'd been too shy to speak to just a few weeks earlier.

For years, Sophia and the M's had hung out in different groups. While Madison and Mia enjoyed the spotlight, Sophia had huddled in the wings. But now, as Fairview Middle School cheerleaders, they were suddenly on the same team.

In some ways, Sophia was even more on the team than Mia. As an alternate, Mia would be cheering at games only if another sixth grader got sick or for some reason had to leave. Still, she had to learn every chant, cheer, and dance so that she could fill in at any time. Luckily

for her and Madison, this meant they could keep spending every second of every afternoon an arm's length apart at the most.

"Good idea. Let's go," said Kendall, linking her arm through Sophia's elbow. "Maybe we can find out what this 'surprise' Madison's been talking about is, too."

Almost immediately afterward, though, Coach Casey blew her whistle — *FWWEEEEEE!* — and called the whole squad to her.

"Break's over!" The coach clapped. "Back to the center. Alternates, line up on the end. Your new captains, Ella and Natasha, are going to lead you all in one-leg snap-ups — otherwise known as kicks."

The two eighth graders jogged to the front of the gym on cue and waved the others into place. Natasha was taller and more muscular, but Ella seemed to take up more space. Her hair burst out of her ponytail in thick, dark rings, and her smile was warm, sunny, and surprising, thanks to the gap between her teeth.

"Let's go! Let's do it!" they cheered as they stretched their arms out to the sides. They locked their elbows tight. "Ready? Arms in T! Fifty kicks to the right!"

Natasha and Ella had just been elected captains on Monday in a landslide. Any eighth grader could run for one of the two captain spots, provided she'd cheered the year before. Five had put their names in and given short speeches to the team explaining why they were the best girls for the job. Sophia had loved what Natasha had said

about wanting to give back as much to the squad as it had given her. "Plus, I know how to be a great big sister, since I have four little sisters of my own!" And how could anyone not have voted for Ella, who had crossed her heart and promised to be "the best cheer captain that Fairview ever had! Not that Jackie and Jordan weren't great last year . . . and Remy and Caitlin before that . . ."

As captains, they got to help the coach lead the squad through stretches and drills. Later — the next week, in fact, when football started — they'd be in charge of leading all the sideline chants and cheers.

". . . forty-nine . . . fifty!" they shouted. "Switch! Now the left!"

After high kicks came calf-busters, which was basically lots and lots and lots and *lots* of bouncing on their toes. Then it was time to practice all the jumps they'd learned so far as a squad. Sophia was really happy with how much better her toe touch had gotten. Her herkie, on the other hand, still had a ways to go.

"Smiles, everyone, smiles!" Coach Casey reminded them as they drilled. "Don't think about the burn. Think about getting your legs UP! And not letting your hands drop down. And think about how strong you're getting. No pain, no gain! Remember those words!"

The coach clapped when they were done. "Very nice, girls! I like what I see! Now, make sure when you're at home to keep practicing. For tomorrow, I want you to focus on pointing your toes. And don't

worry. Those herkies are *nearly* there. Down on the mats, now, ladies. Let's stretch it out, and then I think we can call it a day."

"Oh, Coach!" Madison's hand popped into the air. Her other hand was on her waist.

"Yes, Madison?"

"Did you want to tell everyone about that *thing* my mom talked with you about, you know, before practice today?"

"Of course!" Coach Casey clapped. "How could I forget?" She looked over the squad. *You're going to like this!* her expression said.

Sophia traded raised eyebrows with Kendall, then waited to hear what Coach Casey would say next.

"Everyone, I hope you're all free on Saturday, because Madison's family, the McElroys, has come up with a really great idea! They've most graciously offered to host a barbecue for the whole squad as a way to kick off our new cheer year!"

There was an instant twitter of excitement. The words "tennis court" and "mansion" could be heard.

"You won't want to miss it," said Madison even though it was clear that everyone was already excited about the party.

"Madison's getting a new —" Mia started, but Madison shushed her instantly.

"Don't tell them!" she said coyly. "You'll all see on Saturday."

CHAPTER 2

"Ooh! That's nice!" said Sophia, nodding to the outfit Kendall had just laid out on her bed. Brand-new jeans were embellished with silver thread along the pockets and the sides, and a dark- and light-green striped T-shirt had three-quarter sleeves and a boatneck.

"Better than this one?" asked Kendall, pointing to the outfit she'd put down first. That was cute, too — a white ruffled skirt, a beaded belt, and a lavender embroidered top.

"I don't know." Sophia paused. "Oh, gosh, I like them both." She would have worn either in a heartbeat. "What do *you* think?" she asked Kendall.

Kendall laughed. "I don't know, either. That's why I'm asking you!"

"Well . . ." Sophia picked up the green shirt and held it under Kendall's chin. She cocked her head and frowned. Then she switched the top for the light purple one and leaned the other way. "Both look great on you," she said. "I guess it comes down to what you feel best

in. What kind of first impression do you want to make? I mean, Madison did say, whatever you do, don't look like you're trying too hard. So maybe that means jeans?" She held the shirt up to her own shoulders. "But this is a great top, I have to say."

Madison had been more than happy to give them wardrobe advice after practice. "No sneakers!" she'd warned. "Unless they're high-tops."

Mia had nodded. "Right. Those are okay."

"But better to go with sandals," Madison advised them.

"Or flats," Mia said.

"Right. Of course," Madison agreed.

But when Sophia and Kendall asked M&M what they were wearing, they said they still weren't sure.

"I have *so* many things to choose from." Madison sighed. "Honestly, I don't know *how* I'm going to pick."

"I know, right?" said Mia wearily, as if life were too unfair.

Maybe it really was hard having so much. Sofia certainly didn't know. Her mom had been happy to buy her a first-day-of-school outfit, but one, and only one. And even picking that out hadn't been hard, since there were never that many cute things to choose from at the stores where they shopped.

"Hi, guys. Whatcha doin'?"

Kendall's bedroom door cracked open and a head full of braids peeked in.

"Libby." Kendall groaned. "Seriously? I've told you a million times, you have to *knock*."

"Sorry," said Kendall's nine-year-old sister, although her smile said it wouldn't be the last time she forgot. "I just wasn't sure if you guys heard the ice cream man. He's been parked up the street for a while now. You guys hungry?"

"Really? The ice cream man?" Kendall reached out to turn down her music.

She listened . . . and so did Sophia. . . . The truck's signature song found its way to their ears.

"Want to?" Kendall asked Sophia.

"Yeah, sure," Sophia said.

She laid Kendall's new tops back down on her bedspread. "Thanks for the heads-up, Libby!" Sophia said. She wondered if all little sisters were as cool as Kendall's, or if Kendall was particularly fortunate.

"Wait . . . what's that?" Sophia suddenly heard another tune, but this one was coming from inside the room. In fact, it was coming from her own tote bag. "Oh, hang on," she said. "It's my phone."

It was probably her mom, she figured, calling to tell her she was going to pick her up on her way home from work. This was Sophia's

mom's last week at the nursing home where she'd temped through summer break. The next week, she'd be back at her regular job as Fairview Middle School's resident nurse.

Her mom kept joking about how they were going to be "working together." In fact, it seemed like she talked about it all the time. If she noticed that Sophia tried to change the subject, she didn't let it stop her from changing it back.

Sophia loved her mom a lot. There were more-embarrassing moms out there, for sure. But the whole mom-at-her-middle-school-every-day-all-day thing was beginning to worry her. She could just see her mom doing something like suggesting she brush her teeth after lunch — and not privately, in her office, but right in the middle of the hall. Or worse, Sophia could see her chasing her down to give her a big *I'm so proud of you* hug, somewhere crowded and conspicuous . . . like on the stage in the auditorium.

Those kinds of pictures, plus many more, were springing up all the time in her mind these days. But they burst like bubbles as soon as she found her phone and read the caller's name.

Gwen.

No way! Sophia hadn't talked to Gwen in weeks. She had been gone for most of the summer, first to camp and then to the beach. Sophia suddenly realized she hadn't even told her yet about the whole cheer-tryout thing. Gwen's camp had a no-phone rule, but old-fashioned

letters were okay. Sophia had actually written one after cheer tryouts. . . . It had just never made it into the mail.

"You guys go ahead," Sophia told Kendall and Libby. "It's my friend," she explained. "I bet she just got home from the beach."

"Want us to get you something?" Kendall asked, joining Libby by the door.

"An ice cream sandwich?"

"You got it."

"Need money?" asked Sophia.

"Nah." Libby waved a bill and shook her head. "Already got some from Mom for all of us. But let's hurry, Kendall!" she begged.

They were gone by the time Sophia answered her call. "Hi! Where *are* you? Are you home?" she gushed, flopping down on Kendall's window seat and finally pausing for a response.

"I am," said Gwen in the matter-of-fact voice Sophia had come to know so well. Gwen never sounded too excited, even when she really was. Her emotions got as far as mildly amused, and that was normally where they stopped.

That, and her very straight posture, made some people think she was stuck-up. But really she was just thoughtful and serious.

"So how was the beach?" asked Sophia. "How was the whole family reunion thing? Did your grandmother sing the whole time?"

"Of course she did," said Gwen, whose grandmother Sophia had

met many times. She was a sweet and energetic old lady who, for some reason, preferred to sing instead of talk. "Would you believe she even started to sing about why she loves to sing so much?" Gwen went on.

"Really?" Sophia giggled. "Sing it for me. Please."

"Um. No," Gwen replied dryly. "And personally, I'm not sure so much singing is all that funny," she declared. "I told my mom it could be serious. Some kind of brain thing, perhaps."

"And what did she say?"

"She and my aunts — they think they're hilarious — they started singing then, too, and didn't stop for the rest of the day."

Sophia laughed. "Well, I guess it's not so bad if that's the only thing that drives you crazy on a big family vacation. It could be a whole lot worse."

"Indeed," Gwen said in a deep, dark way that let Sophia know how right she was.

"*What?* What happened?" asked Sophia. Her own summer news would have to wait.

"Well."

"Well what? Go on!"

"I have these cousins. From Milwaukee. They're in high school. We don't see them all that much. I'd seen pictures. But I had no idea how bad it really was."

"How bad *what* was?" asked Sophia, already imagining dozens of terrible, horrible things. But it wasn't like Gwen to get hung up on appearances, no matter how gruesome they might be. She was always the one saying, "Don't judge a book by its cover," after all. (Of course, most of the times she said that, she was talking about actual books.)

"I'll give you a hint," said Gwen. "Rah. Rah. Rah."

Rah, rah, rah? Sophia stared at her feet. She pulled her bangs down to her nose. "Rah, rah, rah?" she slowly repeated.

"They were such *cheerleaders*!" Gwen groaned. "Straight off the sidelines, if you know what I mean. They practiced *all* the time. It was like everything deserved a cheer. 'Give me a *G*. Give me a *W*. Give me an *E*. Give me an *N*.' They woke me up with that every morning. 'Give me a break,' I told them. Can you imagine? So much jumping. So much . . . stuff with the hands. And not for just one, but for *two* excruciating weeks."

Gwen paused for a moan of sympathy from Sophia, but silence seemed to be enough.

"Camp, however, was outstanding. It rained, so I got to play lots of chess. I ran out of books, though," Gwen went on solemnly. "I should have brought another bag, I guess. But enough about me. I thought you were going to write to me and tell me what was going on with you. How was *your* summer? I know your mom had to work. You found things to do to keep you from getting *too* bored, I assume."

"Um . . ." Now Sophia had to say something. But what, she wasn't sure. "Um . . . yeah . . ."

"Well, good," said Gwen after a moment. "So . . . want to come over tomorrow? Or I could come to you." She paused. "Sophia? Are you there? Did I lose you?"

"Yeah, yeah. I'm here. That would be great. But, um, yeah . . . um . . . tomorrow I can't."

"Oh." Sophia could picture Gwen frowning slightly as she waited for her to explain. But how could she give Gwen the reason — "I have cheerleading practice" — after what Gwen had just said? She'd had no doubt, of course, that cheerleading wasn't Gwen's cup of tea. That was mostly why the letter she'd written to Gwen about it was still lying on her desk. But it had never occurred to Sophia that Gwen would look *down* on it like that. She'd been almost excited to surprise her friend with such big, unexpected news. But all of a sudden, she felt like she had to keep it a secret as long as she possibly could.

"Saturday, then?" Gwen asked. "I'm going to this bird talk with my parents in the morning. But maybe in the afternoon?"

"Saturday afternoon? Oh, I can't. I have . . . something I have to do."

Specifically, hang out with a bunch of cheerleaders at the squad barbecue.

"Sunday?" Gwen's voice went up a little, caught somewhere between impatient and confused.

Was she sorry or relieved, Sophia wondered, to have to answer again with a no? At least this time she could say why: "I wish I could, Gwen, but I'm going to my dad's. I'll be there until Monday night."

"Are you saying we're not going to see each other until *Tuesday*, at school?"

"I guess not. . . ." Sophia replied. "Are you . . . nervous about starting middle school?" she asked after a pause.

"Nervous? Not really. Are you?" Gwen asked.

"A little. It's going to be a lot . . . different. Don't you think?"

"Different? Well, yes, I suppose." She could hear the shrug in Gwen's reply. "But I thought we were both tired of elementary school. Think of how much more we're going to learn. And besides, *we're* still the same," she said. "And that's what matters most."

"Right . . ." Sophia sure hoped Gwen would feel the same way when she finally discovered Sophia's big news.

CHAPTER 3

Sophia and her mom drove up to Madison's house on Saturday and parked beside the curb. The wide circular driveway was already full.

"What a pretty house," said Sophia's mom as she opened the driver-side door. She flipped down the sun visor and smoothed her hair back, then climbed out of the car.

Sophia stepped out, too, but more slowly, on account of the object in her lap: a bowl filled with enough guacamole to feed the squad — for life.

"Be careful with that," warned her mom.

"I've got it. Don't worry," Sophia said. "Do you have the chips?"

"Right here," her mom said, reaching into the backseat for a shopping bag.

They followed the blue and white Fairfield balloons along a stone path around the house, to a gate leading into a vast charcoal-scented oasis — better known as Madison's backyard.

"Hello! Hell-*o*!" A pretty woman waved to them from a patio filled with grown-ups, and strode toward them across the grass. A little dog yelped and ran to join her, desperate not to be left behind.

The woman wore a bright blue sundress and white sandals studded with berry-sized jewels. A wide headband kept her wavy blond hair behind earrings that swung with every step. The moon-shaped dimple in one of her cheeks was just like Madison's.

On the patio, a man stepped out, waving, from behind a grill the size of a car. "Howdy!" he called, brandishing an arm-long spatula. Sophia squinted to read his apron: KEEP CALM AND CHEER ON.

"Welcome! Monica, right? So good to see you again!" gushed the woman as she reached them. She leaned in to kiss Sophia's mom on the cheek. "Mindy McElroy. Remember?" She put her hands to her chest and blinked.

"Arf! Arf!" The dog raised himself on his hind legs between them, batting his tiny front paws. Sophia wasn't sure if he was greeting them, too, or begging for someone to have mercy and snip off his metallic blue bow.

"Herkie, down boy," cooed the woman. The dog sat down, then popped back up while Madison's mom continued. "Can you believe it? Time goes so fast!" she told Sophia's mother. "Our little girls going into sixth grade! And cheerleaders! At last! And *you*!" She turned to

Sophia. "Tell me! How excited are you to be on the squad with Madison!"

"Um, very," Sophia told her with a smile she hoped was big enough.

"Well, congratulations! I know those tryouts can be hard! I've been through a few myself, you know. Ooh!" Mrs. McElroy looked down at the bowl Sophia was holding. "Is this what I think it is?" she asked.

"Guacamole?"

"Se ve delicioso! Muchos gracias!" Mrs. McElroy trilled.

"Good Spanish," remarked Sophia's mom, who was a little rusty herself.

Madison's mom shrugged. "What can I say? I spent some time in Texas when I was young. Or should I say *younger*?" She grinned. "Here, honey, let me take that from you." She reached for the heavy bowl, and Sophia happily let it go. "Go have fun. The girls are all over there. And *you*." She nodded to Sophia's mom. "We cheer moms have a *lot* to talk about, so follow me, Monica. Herkie?" She looked down. "Herkie! Bad boy. *No*."

While her mom vainly worked to shake the McElroys' dog off her shin, Sophia headed off to the area Madison's mom had steered her toward. It was a wide open stretch of lawn, where most of the squad already stood. They were gathered around something very interesting . . . and very huge.

"Sophia! You're here!" Several girls noticed her and waved.

"Sophia! Hi!" More girls turned, grinned, and did the same.

Sophia waved back. She realized that it still surprised her to feel so comfortable around all the other girls. Yet from her very first day on the squad, she'd never doubted that it was a place where she belonged. The kids on the chess team had all been nice, and they'd always said "good job" when she won, but it was nothing like cheerleading, which had welcomed her with open arms.

She picked up her pace and suddenly saw just about the last thing she expected to see: a body flying up behind the girls and flipping backward before it disappeared.

"Yay!"

"One more time!"

"You can do it!" the girls cheered. "Go for ten!"

Once again, the body flew up . . . and it flipped the other way this time. Then up it came again, this time scissoring its bare brown arms and legs.

"So*phee*a! Hi! You have to try Madison's trampoline!" it shouted from the sky.

It was Kendall!

Sophia watched her pop back up once more and do a double tuck. By the time Sophia reached the circle, the other girls were making space for Kendall to dismount.

Kendall reached out to hug Sophia as soon as she hopped down. "That was so fun!" she exclaimed. "I love trampolines so much!"

"You're welcome." Madison stepped up with a clipboard and plucked a pen from behind her ear. "Sophia. Good. You're here," she said, checking something off her list.

"Wow. Is this your surprise?" Sophia asked. The trampoline was round, enclosed by a tall net, and almost as big as her room at home.

"Yep. We just got it. *Finally*. To replace our old one, which we wore out in the spring. Well, *we* didn't wear it out," she clarified. She rolled her eyes. "My *father* did."

Mia, who was beside her, giggled. "He fell right through. I was there."

"It was pretty classic," Madison agreed, smiling. "I wish we'd gotten it on video. Oh, well. Now the tramp's off-limits to him. Have you ever tried one before?" she asked Sophia.

"No. Never." She shook her head. "But I've always wanted to."

"Of course you have," said Madison.

"Do we, um, need to sign up?" Sophia asked, pointing to Madison's list.

"Oh, no." Madison shook her head. "*I* put you down. See, you're after Georgia. I'll let you know when it's your turn. It's Sadie's turn now. Where is she? Sadie, get over here. You're up," she called.

Sadie raised her hand and stepped forward, somehow smiling while clearly working hard to chew. "Maybe I should pass — and take my turn a little later," she said finally. "I just ate a hot dog. Well, actually two."

"Already?" Madison frowned.

"I couldn't help it. They smelled *so* good."

Mia nodded knowingly. "Madison's parties always have the best food."

And a lot of it, Sophia thought. Aside from the long, food-filled tables on the patio, there were smaller ones with trays loaded with chips and dips and desserts set out around the yard. Plus a popcorn machine, the old-fashioned-looking kind that rolled around on wheels, was fragrantly huffing and puffing and popping beside a gazebo not far from them. And if Sophia wasn't mistaken . . .

"Is that a frozen yogurt machine?" she asked.

"Mmm-hmm," Madison answered.

"Chocolate *and* vanilla," Mia said.

A teenage girl, slightly taller than Madison, stepped up to it as they spoke. She let go of the hand of a very tall and muscular boy with short, bushy hair. The girl had the same bouncy blond ponytail as Madison, and the same long, strong legs. In fact, she looked like Sophia imagined Madison would look someday in high school.

The girl filled a cup with a mound of vanilla and handed it to the boy. Then she got another and they moved to a table covered with dishes of candy and fruit and syrups, and cans of whipped cream in ice-filled bowls.

"Is that —" Sophia started to ask.

"My sister, Megan. And her boyfriend," Madison confirmed, doodling something on her list.

Megan. Sophia had been hearing about her since tryouts. She was the captain of her high school squad. She'd been a cheer captain in middle school, too. The team still did cheers she had created years earlier.

Sophia and the other girls watched the couple taste each other's yogurts as they strolled toward a garden swing.

"Gross." Sadie giggled.

"I know, right?" said Madison. "And just wait till they start to kiss."

As it turned out, they didn't wait long. Three seconds, approximately.

"*Any*way," said Madison. "Georgia. You can go."

"Let Sophia go before me," said Georgia. "I think I might get some yogurt first."

"Really?" said Sophia. "Okay, Madison?"

Madison thought about it, then nodded and officially revised her list.

"Yay! Great! Get up there!" Kendall urged, pulling the net back for Sophia to climb through. "You should try flipping backward! It's great tumbling practice," she said. "It would be so cool if you could add something to your cartwheel before the first football game next week, don't you think?"

Sophia dropped her chin and looked at Kendall through the curtain of her bangs. Yes. It *would* be cool, she had to agree. But so would, oh, finding a unicorn under her bed.

She loved how encouraging Kendall was, and how happy she always was to help. But Sophia wasn't sure Kendall quite got that what was easy for *her* to do — like back handsprings — was still close to impossible as far as Sophia was concerned. Her body just didn't work that way, though Kendall said if she kept trying, it would come. Sophia was trying, and trying . . . and trying. And falling on her butt a lot.

"Get up there, Sophia. It's so fun!" said Katie, one of the seventh graders on the squad.

"Wait. Hold on." Madison held up her hand.

Sophia froze. "What's wrong?"

"Shoes off." Madison pointed to her feet.

"Oh, right!" Sophia kicked off her flip-flops and took a deep breath. "Good? Okay. Here goes."

She pulled herself up over the blue padded edge of the trampoline and climbed rather clumsily to her feet. Her knees buckled as she

tried to walk toward the middle of the mat, away from the squeaky springs.

"It's easier if you just start bouncing," Kendall called up to her helpfully.

It was true, Sophia realized as she gently bent her legs and allowed the mat to lift her like a wave. She crouched more deeply, and soon she wasn't just bouncing, but jumping, and getting more and more air as she did.

"Whoo! Higher!" The girls below started cheering.

Then someone, maybe Ella, starting calling out jumps:

"Toe touch! . . . Hurdle! . . . Herkie! . . . Pike! . . ."

"Oops," Sophia said, laughing, as she totally messed that one up.

She tried a pike again, though, and this time she got it. Her legs shot straight out and she touched her toes. She was so much more limber than when tryouts started, she thought happily. All that stretching had definitely paid off.

"We need these on the sidelines!" she called down to Kendall between liftoffs. "Then I'd have time to get my feet where they have to go!"

"I know!" Kendall shouted back. "The trampoline makes it so easy, doesn't it! Now try some flips! They're super fun!"

Sophia sprang back into the air and kicked her legs out in a spread eagle. She looked down, amazed at the height she'd built up. It was

actually a little scary . . . or it could be . . . if you let it get to you, she thought. At the same time, though, the idea of a somersault didn't seem all that frightening anymore. In fact, it suddenly seemed natural to try it . . . and almost before she knew it, she tucked and rolled. . . .

"Yeah!"

"Go, Sophia!"

One front somersault later, Sophia landed on the mat on her feet. Briefly. She then stumbled forward onto her hands and knees. Still, that didn't keep her from taking a satisfied bow and setting up for another one. Except this time, instead of rolling her body forward, she grabbed her knees and threw herself back. She closed her eyes, felt her body flip over, and prepared for the rebound.

"Uh-oh!" she heard coming from someone behind her just as she landed — not on her feet, but on the seat of her pants. And not on the trampoline, either, but between the rail around it and the stretchy mesh net.

"Are you okay?"

About twenty hands reached out to catch her, but she wasn't going anywhere. She was wedged in pretty tight, her knees up against her chin.

"I'm fine," she murmured as she wiggled out. It hadn't even hurt, luckily. A slightly bruised ego was about her only injury.

"That was good until the last part," said Kendall. She offered Sophia a hand to help her down.

Sophia took it and hopped to the soft grass, glad to be back on solid land.

"Good thing there was a net!" said Katie.

"And *that's* why we have alternates," Madison declared, turning to Mia.

"Madison!" Katie hissed as others frowned.

"What?" Madison looked around innocently. "It's true," she said. "Not that I want you to get hurt, *of course*, Sophia." She put a hand on her hip. "What kind of person do you think I am?"

CHAPTER 4

On Sunday, Sophia's dad picked her up at home after church. As usual, he called from his car to say he was waiting outside. As usual, her mom handed Sophia the phone so she could answer it.

"Don't you want to say hi?" Sophia asked her, as usual.

Her mom shook her head, like she did every time.

Sophia sighed. It never hurt to try. "Hi, Dad. Be right there," she said into the phone.

She hugged her mom when she hung up. "See you tomorrow, Mom. Be good. Don't do anything I wouldn't do."

Her mom pouted teasingly. "That doesn't leave me very much."

Sophia left with nothing but the book she was reading. She didn't have to pack an overnight bag anymore. She had a set of everything she needed at her dad's apartment. A toothbrush, pajamas, plus some casual clothes. What she didn't have there yet was a real bedroom. When she slept over, they pulled out the couch, but she didn't really

mind that it felt temporary. She wasn't going to stop hoping, no matter how divorced her parents were now, that one day they'd come to their senses and her dad would move back home.

Besides, since Sophia's dad traveled half the year, she wasn't there all that much, anyway. He was a professional baseball scout, which meant he zigzagged all over the country checking out different baseball players. All spring, and a *lot* of the summer, Sophia hardly saw him at all. But in the fall and winter he made sure they got together once a week. More, if possible.

Sophia's parents had been separated for over a year but officially divorced for just a month. She remembered the day they signed the papers, the week before cheer tryouts began. Her mom had bought a new dress for "the occasion" and kept it on when she got home. For dinner, she made lasagna, Sophia's favorite, even though it was ninety degrees outside. When she started pouring sparkling cider, Sophia finally had to speak up.

"Are we *celebrating*?" she asked, a little angry. But mostly confused.

"No." Her mom had sighed. "Just marking the start of a new stage in our lives."

"Divorce" was a stage Sophia didn't like to think about, though it hadn't been much different from "Separation" so far. During the week, it was Sophia and her mom, cooking together, watching movies,

and, when her mom wasn't working, hanging out at their little neighborhood pool. And on the weekends he was home, it was Sophia-Dad time, which meant ordering takeout, playing chess, and sports, sports, *sports.*

Watching, that is. Not playing.

Over the years, Sophia's dad had signed her up for just about everything that involved printed T-shirts, special footwear, and round objects she could hit, kick, or bounce. Soccer, baseball, softball, basketball, tennis, lacrosse. Her dad even took her to play golf — once. That was the most torturous, by far.

Sophia knew how important sports were to her dad, and she'd tried to please him by playing along. But he kept saying the point was to "have fun out there," and for her it never was.

Finally, they gave up on Sophia's playing any game except one. Chess. Her dad had taught her to play back in kindergarten and it had been "their" game ever since.

"Hey, Soph!" he said as she climbed into the front seat. "I missed you. Hey, you look taller. Have you grown?"

"Dad," she groaned. Taller? Really? "It's only been a few weeks."

"I know. But you look . . . different. Did you get a haircut?"

"Dad." She had to smile. She hadn't cut her hair in *years.* "Dad, you know you should have come in and said hi to Mom. I don't know why you don't. *She* just got a haircut and she looks really pretty. . . .

Hey, what's this?" As she reached to buckle her seat belt, she noticed a bag tucked in by the latch. "For me?" she said, hoping.

"And who else would it be for?"

Her dad always brought her something from wherever he went. And it wasn't just some guilty, divorced-dad thing — like soda with dinner, which totally was. He'd brought back presents for as long as she could remember, since she was a little girl.

She picked up the bag and peeked inside before pulling out a hat. It was a navy blue baseball cap with a red brim and a red chess knight, her favorite piece, embroidered on the crown.

She put it on, grinning, and tugged the brim down, modeling it for him.

"I love it! Thanks!" she said.

"It's from Fairleigh Dickinson," he informed her, "in New Jersey, in case you're interested."

Still smiling, she shook her head. "Not really," she teased.

"I didn't think so. But there's more. Don't stop. Keep digging in."

She did and unfurled a navy T-shirt with the same red chess-knight logo on the chest. She could see it was made especially for a girl and came in a little at the waist.

She held it in front of her. "*Very* cool."

"Oh, good. As soon as I saw it, I thought of you."

Sophia leaned over to kiss his bristly cheek. He smelled much better than his car. If her mom could just get this close to her dad, thought Sophia, she was sure to fall back in love.

"So." Her dad started the engine and checked the side mirror as he eased out of the parking space. "Middle school next week. Wow. Excited?" he asked.

Sophia pulled her new hat down farther. "A little. Yeah, I guess so. A little excited. A little scared."

"Of what?"

"Oh, new people. New teachers. Changing classes. What if I get lost?"

(Plus Gwen's finding out she was a cheerleader. There was that now, too, of course.)

"Ah, what if you do get lost? . . . Good question. You could leave a trail of breadcrumbs behind you," her dad joked.

Sophia rolled her eyes and reached to turn on the radio. A laugh, or even a smile, would just encourage him, she knew.

"Well, what are you looking forward to?" he went on. "Let's concentrate on that. Hey, do they have a chess team? Have you checked into that yet?"

"No," Sophia said as she settled on a station that was coincidentally playing their halftime dance song. "Actually . . ." She sat back

and turned to her dad. She'd been waiting to tell him in person and not over the phone. "I have some kind of big news."

"Really? What?"

"I tried out for a different team."

"You did?" He looked at her, wide-eyed, then turned back to the road.

"Uh-huh. And I made it." She could tell she was smiling too much.

"You *what*?"

Sophia was glad they'd come to a stoplight, or her dad might have hit the brakes in the middle of the street.

"Well . . . while you were away, I decided to try out for cheerleading. And somehow I did it — I made the squad!"

"*Cheer*leading?" His face, which had been electrified, slowly lost its charge. "Cheerleading," he said again slowly.

Beep, beep!

The light turned green and the car behind them blew its horn.

"Yes. Cheerleading." Sophia knew her face changed, too, from *I did it!* to *What's wrong*?

"Well, congratulations, I guess," her dad said, facing forward and moving, at last. "But why cheerleading?" he added a few seconds later. "What in the world made you want to do that?"

"I don't know. . . ." Sophia had to swallow — two times — before she could go on. "I mean, I do. I thought it sounded like fun. And I

thought it would be a good chance now, when I'm starting middle school, to try something totally new. And to be part of a group. Chess was fun, but we all did our own thing. *You're* the one, after all, Dad, who's always saying how teams are so great."

"Yeah." He nodded. "I know. But I meant a *team*. As in a *sport*."

"Are you serious, Dad?" She turned to stare at him now. "Omigosh. It *is* a sport." She heard her voice rise and felt her cheeks flush. "You should see how hard we practice. And how many skills we've already learned. As opposed to those baseball players of yours" — she crossed her arms — "who just stand around for hours, spitting and chewing gum."

Her dad laughed.

"Hey, maybe that's why I look different," she added, flexing her bicep.

Her dad reached out to test it and nodded, looking impressed.

"And your mom was okay with this?"

Sophia nodded. "Totally. She thinks it's great."

"And it's fun?"

"It's so fun," she told him. "I mean, the practices are long — and hard, like I said. And I still have a lot to learn. But the girls are so nice. And the coach is awesome. We're going to be cheering at the first home football game, next Friday. Will you be here? Do you think you could come?"

He turned onto the highway. "Next Friday . . . Yeah, I can be here. When? Right after school?"

"Right after. Yes." She leaned toward him eagerly. "So you'll come?"

"Of course I'll come," he said. "You know me." He winked. "Always up for some football."

Sophia gave him a "Ha-ha. Very funny," just to be generous. Then she sat back with a sigh.

Dad's going to see me cheer! she thought immediately. But then something else even better followed that: *Dad's going to see* Mom*! They'll be together for two whole hours!* Sophia had already been enjoying cheerleading, but suddenly she loved it even more. If it could get her parents back together, it would *really* change her life. That would more than make up for the explaining she still had to do to Gwen.

CHAPTER 5

The rest of the weekend seemed to fly by, even though Sophia tried to make it last.

Sunday it was just Sophia and her dad. They ordered Chinese food and played chess — two long games, both of which Sophia won. Sure, her dad was watching football *and* baseball on TV at the same time, but Sophia still felt satisfied.

On Monday, they went to a real baseball game, and then to a picnic at the house of one of her dad's friends. She ate more hot dogs that weekend than the whole rest of the summer combined, she realized by the end.

She got back home very full and slightly sunburned and later than her mom had planned.

"Would it be so hard for your dad to remember sunscreen?" Her mom sighed. "And maybe a watch, once in a while."

Sophia shrugged and seized the chance to say, sincerely, "See? Dad *needs* you, Mom."

There was just enough time to get her first-day outfit ready before bed: her new black jeans and a turquoise top that came with its own matching camisole. She wished she had cute flats or sandals to go with it, but sneakers would just have to do. The only other options she had were flip-flops and way-too-dressy black church shoes. Oh, and cheer shoes, of course, but under no circumstance could she wear those. They were for game day only. That was the rule.

She laid the clothes across her footboard, then glanced at the bag she'd gotten from her dad. She thought about the chess shirt inside, and grabbed the bag and dumped it out. She switched it for the new top and approved it with a quick, decisive nod. Not only was it cute, but Gwen was going to love it, too.

"You look adorable! Nice shirt. Where'd you get it?" her mom said the next morning when Sophia came out dressed and anxious to leave.

"You like it?" Sophia saw another opportunity to talk up her dad. "*Dad* gave it to me," she said. "Hey! I bet he could get one for you, too, if you called him and asked!"

"Hmm . . . maybe . . ." Her mom poured a little more coffee into the oversize mug Sophia had painted for her mom's birthday years

before. The handle had broken off several times and been superglued back on. Her mom still used it every day, though, and swore she always would. If only they made superglue for parents . . . *How great would that be?* Sophia thought.

Her mom took a sip and smiled at Sophia. "Eat. I made sweet rolls. Then, if you want, I'll braid your hair."

"French braid?" Sophia grinned.

"Whatever you want," her mom said.

They got to school just as the very first buses were pulling in. The sidewalk was sprinkled with kids who lived close and could walk. Some traveled in clusters and some by themselves.

"I think I'll . . . wait," Sophia said as her mom — *bloop-bloop* — locked the car and dropped her keys into her bag.

Her mom frowned for a second, then nodded, understanding. "*Oh* . . . you don't want to walk in with *me*," she said.

"Sorry." Sophia reached out and hugged her mom quickly. "I'm not trying to be mean."

"No, no. I get it. This is middle school. Kids don't walk in with their moms." She kissed Sophia on the forehead and took a step away. "You know where to go, right? Turn left when you go in —"

"I know, Mom. Turn left. Look for the lists of homerooms. Don't worry. I'll find my way. And didn't you say there'd be plenty of teachers there helping us all figure out where to go?" Frankly, after going

to school every day for the past week for cheerleading practice, finding her way to her first-period classroom was among the least of Sophie's concerns.

"Shall I meet you here after school?" her mom asked.

"Well, I have practice, remember," Sophia said. She patted her new backpack, which contained her workout gear: shorts, a T-shirt, and her white cheer shoes.

"Oh, right. I'll wait in my office, then. Meet me there, okay?"

"Sounds good," said Sophia. She waved. "Thanks. Have a good day."

"*You* have a good day," her mom said as she finally turned away.

Her mom looked pretty in her summery shirtdress, Sophia thought. It was a welcome change from those shapeless, drab-colored nursing-home scrubs. Sophia watched her mom reach the front doors and slip into the school. Okay. She slung her backpack onto her shoulder. Now it was her turn.

"Sophia."

"Sophia!"

"Gwen! Kendall!"

Sophia hurried into room 110, excited by what she knew she'd find. She'd felt as if she'd won the homeroom lottery when she saw Kendall's *and* Gwen's names below hers on the class list in the hall.

And there they were, already, wandering around the empty desks.

The room was plain and a little disappointing. The words *Mrs. Williams, 6th Grade Homeroom* were written in large letters across the board. The teacher must have been out directing new students, however, because just kids were in the room so far.

Besides her, Gwen, and Kendall, there were two boys Sophia didn't recognize and another, Jack Kneeley, who had been in her class every year since first grade but hadn't spoken to her since fourth.

Kendall ran up right away, so Sophia hugged her first. Gwen, who walked, got the second hug, plus a happy third.

"This is so great! We're all in the same homeroom together!" Sophia said, giddy with relief. "Gwen, this is Kendall. Kendall, this is Gwen."

The girls smiled and nodded at each other, while Sophia studied Gwen's face. "Wait. Something's missing," she said.

Gwen blinked and blushed beneath the summer color in her cheeks.

"Did you get contacts?"

"I did." Gwen shrugged. "What can I say? I guess I thought middle school was a good time for a change."

So true, thought Sophia. "I know what you mean. You look great." Sophia turned to Kendall. "Gwen's worn glasses since . . . forever," she explained.

"Since first grade, to be precise," said Gwen. "Let's not exaggerate."

"Kendall just moved here this summer from New York City," Sophia informed Gwen. "Gwen's been there," she told Kendall. "Once, Gwen? Or more?"

"Just once," said Gwen. "Last year. But I really want to go back. We didn't do the one thing I *most* wanted to do."

"What was that?" Kendall asked. "Go to the American Girl Store?"

"Hardly," Gwen assured her. Her naked eyes widened at the thought. "I wanted to see the Metropolitan Opera. Have you been? Is it awesome?"

"I don't know," said Kendall, who'd never gone herself. "I had a babysitter once who was a dancer and was in the chorus sometimes, though. Let me know if you go back and I'll call her. She could get tickets for you, I bet."

"Thanks," said Gwen, brightening and even looking excited — for her. "I don't know when we'll go back, but I'll *definitely* tell you if we do. So. Do you play chess?" she asked Kendall hopefully.

"You know, I've played, but not very much. . . ."

"Well, I bet you could still join the chess team if you wanted to," Gwen said. She smiled at Sophia. "With us. Nice T-shirt, by the way."

"Thanks," Sophia said very softly as Kendall's eyebrows arched.

"Chess team?" Sophia could feel Kendall's eyes on her, though her own eyes were on her shirt. "Gosh . . . I don't know if we'll have time," Kendall went on.

"Why not — Uh-oh. Don't look now," Gwen suddenly said. "But guess who and who just walked in." She was looking between Sophia and Kendall, whose backs were to the door. "M&M," she murmured. "Together. Of course."

Sophia looked up to see Gwen roll her eyes as Kendall spun around. Then she watched Gwen's eyes grow wider while her jaw started to drop. There was no time for Sophia to do anything to prepare Gwen for Madison's and Mia's bounding up.

"Kendall! Hi! Sophia! *Ooh*, you got some sun!" Madison declared, hugging them each. "Oh, but your hair looks so pretty! You have to show me how to do it exactly that way! Okay?"

"Yes, you have to!" echoed Mia, elbowing in for her own hugs. "And then we can *all* do it that way! Won't that be cute?!" she exclaimed.

"Totally." Madison nodded. "Cool T-shirt . . ." She eyed Sophia's top. "Whose team?" she asked, then she giggled. "Oh, who cares if it's not ours."

"What do you think of *our* outfits?" Mia asked, striking a pose.

They matched. Almost perfectly. From their layered tops, to their floral skirts, to their ballet flats with ribbon bows. The only difference was in the color of their backpacks. Madison's was pink with purple trim, while Mia's was the exact opposite.

"You guys look great," said Kendall.

"Yeah, you do," Sophia heard herself say. She was way more focused, though, on how Gwen was staring at her as if she'd sprouted two new heads.

"Thanks! Look at us all in the same homeroom!" Madison turned to Mia, and they shared a squeal and their own bubbly embrace.

"I hope you guys had a good time on Saturday," said Madison.

"It was *so* fun," Kendall said.

"And you weren't sore or anything," Madison asked Sophia, "after your little . . . you know what?"

"No. I'm fine." Sophia shook her head. Her eyes carefully avoided Gwen's.

"Good. You know I was totally joking, right, about Mia getting your spot?"

"Of course she does," said Mia, linking her arm with Madison's.

"Just checking," said Madison. "So." She pointed to the first line of desks and set her backpack down on Gwen's. "These look good, I guess. *This* will be *our* row."

"Yours?" Gwen finally spoke up. Her eyes jumped from the desk to Madison. Her hands shifted to her hips.

Madison's head swiveled in Gwen's direction for the first time since she'd walked in. "Oh, Gwen, right? Hi. You look different," Madison said. "So, yeah. If you don't mind. This row will be for cheerleaders," she continued, tilting her head to explain. "Feel free, of course, to sit anywhere else," she went on diplomatically. "Oh! And that reminds me, *cheerleaders*!" Her focus clicked away from Gwen as if she were a channel with nothing on. "Be sure to get to lunch as fast as you can today. Okay? I'm serious."

"Yes," said Mia. "It's important. We have to get the best table for the squad."

Gwen's mouth was tightly closed by then, and straight as a line. But without any glasses to hide behind, her eyes spoke loud and clear. They were practically yelling, in fact, at Sophia: *You're a* cheerleader? *Since when?*

I can explain, Sophia's eyes tried their best to reply. But she knew she had to say something out loud.

"Uh . . . hang on, Madison, about these seats . . . uh, Gwen was sitting in this one." She patted the desk with Madison's bag, which also still held Gwen's.

Madison glanced from her to the desk to Mia, then back at the desk. "Oh. Okay."

Mia pointed to the next row. "We'll just sit here," she said.

"Sure. Okay. Fine."

Sophia watched Madison move her backpack and weakly smiled at Gwen. Then she held her breath and waited. . . . Gwen, however, did not smile back.

CHAPTER 6

Lunch.

If homeroom was awkward, this was even worse. Instead of looking at Sophia like she didn't recognize her anymore, Gwen had switched to completely ignoring her.

After Sophia had saved her a seat and everything!

Madison and Mia had already staked out a table in the middle of the cafeteria.

"Perfect?" they asked each other.

"Perfect!" they agreed.

It was long enough for the whole squad, but since each grade ate separately, they needed only seven seats. Sophia let Madison and Mia pick theirs — in the center, naturally. Then she put her tray on the end, next to Kendall's, and scanned the crowd for Gwen.

She saw her walk out of the lunch line behind Jack Kneeley and pause and look around. Sophia waved and pointed to the empty place beside her. There was a whole open section, in fact. But if Gwen noticed,

she didn't let on. Her eyes barely skimmed Sophia's head. After a second, she waved to a table by the window where Sophia saw several other old friends from fifth grade. She recognized Lacy and Hannah and funny Josh, whose hair had grown curly and *long*. Sophia watched Gwen march, chin up, to join them, and felt a frown pull her own face down.

"What's wrong?" asked Kendall.

"Hmm? Oh, nothing . . ." Sophia bent her head to study her meal. Chicken tenders. Corn. An apple. Eh. She'd hoped for something better, but middle school lunch wasn't much different from elementary school lunch, it seemed. What *was* different was that she wasn't eating with Gwen for the first time in five years.

"So when?"

"Is it hard?"

"So*fee*a?"

"Huh?" Sophia sensed something and looked up to see twelve cheerleader eyes on her. "What?" The girls all seemed to be waiting patiently for her.

"When can you show us how to do that *braid*?" asked Madison, who was clearly repeating words she'd already said a couple of times.

"Oh, this?" Sophia touched the delicate twist that came over her head like a headband, then fell loose down the side. "It's just a waterfall braid. It's easy. My mom did it for me this morning, but you can totally do it yourself."

"Well, then let's all do it! Tomorrow," proclaimed Madison. "At practice, you can do a little demo for us and all the other girls. Ooh, I can't wait till Friday — can you guys? We all get to wear our uniforms!"

"When do we get them?" asked Georgia.

"Today," said Madison. "I hope."

"I hope I can wear mine, too," Mia said as worry spread across her face.

"Omigosh! I hope so, too!" Madison reached for Mia's hand.

It was clear the idea of not dressing alike was more than they could comprehend.

Luckily, things quickly happened to take their minds off their fear. After all, it *was* lunch. And they *were* M&M. Before Sophia knew it, their table was surrounded by a feeding frenzy of other kids. What was most surprising to Sophia was to be in the middle of it with them.

The empty seats around her promptly filled with girls who knew, or knew *of*, M&M.

"This is *technically* the cheerleader table," Madison made sure to inform them all.

Sophia instantly expected to feel awkward and have to explain why she was there. But right away, girls who'd barely spoken to her just the spring before were acting as if they were old, familiar friends.

And so did girls she'd never met before, who came from other schools. As far as first-day-of-sixth-grade lunches went, she couldn't have asked for much more. Sophia should have been enjoying it. But instead she was missing Gwen.

Sophia hadn't wanted to be popular. What she'd wanted was to be part of a team. And yes, she'd wanted to be known for something in middle school besides being smart and good at chess and spelling bees. She'd had this idea that trying something totally different would help her grow up and, as her mom said, "spread her wings." But she didn't want to end up a different person. She wanted a lot of things to stay just the same. Like her best friend — but Gwen suddenly seemed a world away.

She glanced at Gwen's table — again — and wondered what Gwen was talking about over there.

Oh, why should she wonder? She bet she already knew. If Gwen was talking about anything, it was probably *her.* And how she'd sneaked off and turned into a "cheerleader type" over the summer behind Gwen's back. And how Sophia probably thought she was so great now that she was hanging out with M&M.

At least, that's what Sophia guessed she would have been thinking if she were sitting in Gwen's chair.

She wished she could show Gwen that cheerleaders weren't a certain "type" of girl. They were all different, like everyone else. Kendall,

for example, had tried out because she was new and wanted to make friends before school started — which she definitely had. And Georgia, who was a dancer — ballet and tap — was told by a friend in seventh grade that the squad danced a lot, as well as cheered. Then there was Chandler, who had tried out because she really wanted to cheer for her twin brother, who was going to be on the football team. And Sadie, smiling Sadie, who, Sophia had just found out at the barbecue, lived outside town on a farm. Her parents took in all sorts of animals that needed homes — like horses that were blind and goats that couldn't stand up. Plus, when someone had as happy a face as Sadie did, it just made sense to join the squad.

Then, of course, there was Madison. And Mia. But they were the exception rather than the rule.

Brrriiinnnngg.

The bell rang and tables shook and screeched as kids got up to leave. Sophia looked down at the pile of untouched chicken tenders still on her tray. She had hours of school to go and cheerleading practice after that. She grabbed one and dutifully put it in her mouth, knowing she'd be starving by the time she got home.

"You have math next, right?" said Kendall, leaning over.

Sophia stood up and nodded. "Uh-huh. Let's go."

"Great. Wow . . . you didn't eat much. I thought the food was pretty good. Definitely better than what they gave us back in New York."

"Really?" That was too bad. Sophia picked up her apple, unzipped her backpack, and carefully rolled it in. Then she grabbed her tray to clear it. "I just lost track of time, I guess."

They made their way out of the cafeteria just as the seventh graders were filing in. Gwen slipped right past them, through the doorway, silver-blue eyes straight ahead.

"Hey, there goes Gwen," said Kendall, nodding.

"Oh . . . yeah," Sophia said. She watched and was a little relieved to see Gwen head off to the right instead of to the left with them.

"She didn't know you were a cheerleader, did she?" guessed Kendall.

"No," Sophia confessed.

"You didn't tell her?"

"I *was* going to," said Sophia, "but then she started to talk about her cousins who were cheerleaders and how dumb she thought they were, and, I don't know, I chickened out."

"But you knew you'd have to tell her eventually," said Kendall. "I mean, you weren't going to quit or anything, were you?"

"No," Sophia assured her. "I just thought I'd wait, you know, until we got to school." She sighed. "I guess I blew it. But I never thought it would make her so mad. . . ." She supposed she should have known better. It was one of the first things she learned in chess: before you moved, you always thought two or three turns ahead.

"You should talk to her," said Kendall. "Hey, is this our room?"

They stopped in front of an open door and Sophia read the number on the side: 133. A sign taped below it advertised MRS. DAVIS + 6TH GRADE = MATH.

Sophia's eyes met Kendall's, and they each took a deep breath as they walked in.

"Welcome! I'm Mrs. Davis. Please, take a seat wherever you like."

The teacher at the board smiled at them broadly, revealing an impressive set of teeth. Her face looked young, though her hair was gray — and so short that she could have been bald the day before.

Sophia followed Kendall's lead to two desks by the window. Pots of yellow flowers lined the sill. The window was open and the smell of cut grass blew in on a warm breeze.

Kendall peered out as Sophia set her bag on the floor. "Hey, Sophia!" she said. "I think that's your mom out there. Who's that guy she's with?"

CHAPTER 7

Mrs. Davis might have been the best teacher ever. Or she might have been the worst. Sophia had no idea, because all she could think about the whole way through math class was her mother . . . and that *guy* who'd been with her.

It was a man she'd never seen before. But her mom sure seemed to know him well. Well enough to take his hand to climb down from the bleachers. And well enough to laugh at whatever he said. And well enough to take off her shoe and show him where someone at the nursing home had run over her with a wheelchair.

"Who is it?" Kendall had asked Sophia — again — before class began.

All Sophia could do was shake her head and shrug. "I have no idea."

She knew as much as Kendall did. That he had dark hair. And glasses. The really thick black kind. And that he had no idea about

fashion, since he was wearing sneakers with a plaid shirt and a skinny tie.

She had a feeling he was younger than her dad, but it was hard to tell. At least he didn't have as much gray hair.

They'd clearly just finished lunch when Kendall saw them, and were ready to go inside. Sophia looked around for other teachers. But there was no one else in sight.

As they walked off, Sophia's eyes followed them, and the top half of her body, too.

"Lovely day, isn't it?"

Sophia whipped her head around to face Mrs. Davis and her teeth.

The teacher laid a textbook the size of Sophia's mattress on her desk with a gentle *thud*.

"It's hard to get used to being cooped up inside again, I know," Mrs. Davis said. "Believe me, if I could hold class outside on gorgeous days like this, I would."

Then she moved on and Sophia sighed, relieved the teacher had misunderstood. Math was one of her favorite subjects, and she would have hated for the teacher to get the wrong first impression of her. But what if she had to watch the same scene every day? Sophia suddenly thought. She'd never be able to concentrate on fractions or percentages.

Sophia could give the next class, history, only half of her attention. The memory of her mom and that guy walking back together from lunch was like a loud, long commercial that kept interrupting the teacher's show. But Sophia's last period, science, gave her something else to think about, at least. That was because two seconds after she walked in, Gwen appeared.

They both read the board.

WELCOME TO SCIENCE.

STEP 1: FIND A LAB PARTNER.

STEP 2: FIND A LAB STATION.

STEP 3: PERFORM THE EXPERIMENT.

STEP 4: OBSERVE! OBSERVE! OBSERVE!

STEP 5: SHARE YOUR RESULTS.

This teacher, Ms. Drakoulias, according the sign outside her classroom, wore a white lab coat, like a TV doctor, and shiny black combat boots. She leaned on her desk, grinning and motioning to the board as more and more kids streamed through the open door.

Sophia waited a moment for Gwen's eyes to find hers, but Gwen seemed determined to keep them away. For an instant, Sophia thought, *Fine, whatever.* Then, at last, their eyes met and she waved.

She walked over to Gwen. "Be my lab partner?"

Gwen shifted her backpack. "Okay."

"Sophia!" Sophia turned, and there was Madison, calling to her and bounding up. "Yay! We're together! So! How's the first day gone for you?"

"Oh . . . good . . . fine," Sophia told her. She didn't feel like saying too much more. "You?" she asked.

Madison huffed a little and flicked her hair back. "Well, it could have been a lot better. They got Mia's and my schedules *all* wrong."

"She's not in this class?" asked Sophia. She confirmed it by glancing around.

"No. Or my last period, either," Madison said, adding a sob.

"Oh, wow. That's too bad," said Sophia.

Madison sighed. "I know. But it's okay. I'm going to have my dad fix everything tomorrow." Her eyes shifted to the board over Sophia's shoulder. "Hmm . . . I guess you'll have to be my lab partner today."

As soon as Madison said that, Gwen's mouth stiffened. Sophia knew she had to speak up.

"Uh . . . I'm sorry, Madison. I can't. Gwen . . . me . . ." She waved her hand between them. "We're partners already, I'm afraid."

Madison said nothing for a moment. Her mouth opened slightly but then closed. "Cheerleaders usually stick together for stuff like this," she said finally. "Just so you know . . . But it's just for one day, I guess." She shrugged. *"Sadie!"* She noticed the other girl walking in

smiling, and waved to her with both hands. "Yoo-hoo! Sadie! You're my lab partner! Get over here!"

"Come on." Sophia touched Gwen's elbow and pulled her toward a table where an experiment was set up for them to do. All she saw, though, were two balls — a Ping-Pong ball and a softball — along with a textbook and a piece of cardboard that were equally wide and long.

Gwen was still shaking her head about something.

"What?" Sophia said.

"You. You're a *cheerleader*. Since *when*? And *why*?" Gwen asked.

They were the questions Sophia had been waiting for. Still, she felt like they came at her out of the blue. "I don't know. . . ." she started meekly.

"Well, it didn't just happen," Gwen replied.

No . . . Sophia shrugged. It didn't. But would Gwen understand? She hoped so.

"I got a flyer about it in the mail this summer," she said. "While you were at camp. And, well . . . I don't know . . . it sounded like fun. And it was something to do — since you weren't around. And so . . ." She took a breath. "I decided to try out."

"And you made it?"

Sophia nodded.

"And you didn't tell me?"

Sophia bit her lip. "Well, you didn't tell me about your contacts."

"That's a little different," said Gwen.

She was right, Sophia knew. "I was going to."

"But you didn't." Gwen said this so softly that Sophia almost didn't hear her.

It wasn't until then — that very moment — that Sophia understood. Gwen wasn't mad that she was a cheerleader. She was mad that Sophia hadn't shared it with her.

"Oh, Gwen, I'm really sorry," Sophia said quickly. "I *knew* I should have mailed the letter I wrote when it happened. And then I was all ready to tell you last week on the phone . . . but then you started to talk about your cousins, and I just couldn't tell you after that."

"Why not?" asked Gwen.

"Well . . . I was afraid . . ."

"Of what?"

"Of you . . . I was afraid you'd think *I* was as ridiculous as they were."

"Oh . . ." Gwen's mouth formed a tiny o, which she sucked in slowly.

Sophia cocked her head and waited for Gwen to see her point.

"Well," Gwen said finally. "It is *cheerleading,* after all." Sophia could tell Gwen was half joking — but half very serious, too.

"Honestly, it's not like you think," Sophia hurried to tell her. "Really. It's not all rah-rah-rah. It's actually fun. It's like a sport, but kind of like a dance class, too. And we work really hard. And everyone on the team — seventh and eighth graders, too — is really, really nice. Like Kendall! She's great. And I know she liked you, too. And who knows if I would have met her otherwise."

"Yeah . . . but . . ." Gwen lifted her eyebrows and cut her eyes to Madison across the room.

"Even her. When you get to know her, she's really not that bad." Sophia paused, then had to smile. "Okay, yes, she's still part of M&M." She leaned in a little closer to Gwen and looked straight into her eyes. "Just because I'm on the squad doesn't mean I've changed, Gwen. The only thing that's different is that I can do a cartwheel now."

She grinned, then straightened her mouth out to look as serious as she could. "You know what I think?" she went on.

"What?"

"I think next year *you* should see what it's like for yourself and try out for the squad."

"HA!" A howl of laughter that made every head in the room whirl around suddenly burst out of Gwen. She covered her mouth, looking just as surprised as the rest of the science class.

Ms. Drakoulias rose from the edge of her desk and pointed at

them both. "These experiments aren't going to perform themselves. We don't have time for class clowns in science. More lab work. Fewer jokes."

"Yes, ma'am."

Class clowns. They looked at each other. That was the first time a teacher had ever called them *that*.

They both nodded stiffly and reached for the paper with *GRAVITY!* written across the top.

That was when Sophia noticed how all around them, kids were starting to climb onto tables and chairs. She skimmed the experiment instructions and realized their job was to drop two things at the same time and "observe" them as they fell.

After ten noisy minutes, they had pretty much proved without a doubt that things fell at the same speed, because of gravity, no matter how much, or how little, they weighed. Something both Sophia and Gwen had proven before, actually, in a summer science camp.

"And who do we have to thank for this significant discovery?" asked Ms. Drakoulias after each group had shared their results.

Gwen and Sophia raised their hands together. Theirs were the only hands up in the room. The teacher pointed to them, almost reluctantly, as if she wasn't sure they were serious.

"Yes?"

"Galileo Galilei," they said at the same time.

Ms. Drakoulias nodded, looking satisfied and pleased. "Very good! A lot of kids go right to Sir Isaac Newton and his apple and forget that Galileo came first. Now, if you'll take a seat, I want to show you a video about gravity that I think will really blow your mind."

It was the perfect way to end the day — and not just because the class was so great, but because the wall between Sophia and Gwen had come down.

Gwen even understood when Sophia explained she couldn't come over after school.

"I have to say that I still don't see the appeal," she said, "but I guess it must be fun if you're so eager to practice every day."

They left the science room and stood in the hall saying good-bye until Sophia noticed the clock. She had to be in the gym by 3:15. Sharp.

"See you tomorrow," she told Gwen. "Or call me tonight."

Gwen smiled and shook invisible pom-poms. "Go, Falcons. Have fun."

Sophia waved and hurried off around the corner. Suddenly, a door opened on her right. A dark-haired man stepped out and began to walk in the direction she'd come from.

She recognized the glasses first. Then the shirt. Then the skinny tie.

Him! she thought as he turned the corner — the guy she'd seen outside.

She looked to see what room he'd come out of. But it was the boys' bathroom. That didn't help.

That was when she heard Gwen's voice down the hall. "Hello, Mr. Judd," she said.

CHAPTER 8

Who was *Mr. Judd*?

Sophia was dying to find out. Unfortunately, she knew solving that mystery would have to wait. Coach Casey had made it very clear that being late was N-O-T O-K. "They might take excuses in track, but not on my squad," she had said.

Sophia made it to the gym with just enough time to get to the locker room and change. All the new textbooks she'd collected had crushed the workout clothes she'd brought. The T-shirt she'd packed was even so wrinkled that she decided it was better just to keep her knight shirt on.

FWWWEEEEE!!!

Coach Casey's whistle sounded as Sophia jogged out and hopped to attention in her usual spot.

Kendall was already in her own place, beside Sophia. She turned to Sophia and sighed. "Phew! I'm glad to be somewhere, at last, where everything's not totally new. Aren't you?"

Sophia nodded. Kendall was so right. First days were exciting, but exhausting, too.

"Hello, ladies!" The coach clapped. "How was school?"

All kinds of answers were lobbed back — from groans to "So much fun!"

Sophia went with a plain "good." She probably would have said, "I'm glad it's almost over," if she'd had more time to think.

Coach Casey smiled. "Well, I hope you all found your classes. It was pretty quiet in the library, I have to say. Now, of course, it's time to make some noise!" She paused and put her hand to her ear.

"YEAH!" everyone cheered.

"That's my squad!" Coach Casey called out, clapping again. "Now, we have a *lot* to do, including something I know — or at least I *hope* — you've all been waiting for. . . . But first! We have a guest who needs no introduction — unless you're new to the squad," she went on, "in which case he probably does."

She turned and held out one arm to a man wearing blue shorts and a white polo shirt and standing by the far gym wall. Like Coach Casey, he had a whistle on a lanyard around his neck. And like her, he looked like he knew how to use it to make kids perform.

"Girls, may I present Coach Saunders, our Falcons football coach!" Coach Casey circled her arm to wave the man over. As he approached, she applauded, and the rest of the squad did, as well. "Coach, may I

present your new Falcon cheerleaders." She spread her arms out proudly toward the squad. "Girls, how 'bout you show Coach Saunders what you've got? Ella? Natasha?" She motioned the captains up to the front. "Let's give him a taste of what's to come!"

Eagerly, Ella and Natasha snapped to clean position, arms arrow-straight down, facing the squad. "Ready?" they called as all the other girls copied their moves. The captains' hands snapped to their hips, and so did the squad's.

"Let's Go!" Natasha yelled.

Let's Go. That was a good one, Sophia thought. It was one of the first chants they'd learned. And it was easy. Which was good because Coach Saunders looked as hard to impress as their own coach.

"Let's go, Falcons!"

Natasha called the first line solo, then everyone joined her for four claps. Together, they chanted the next lines, bending their elbows and then punching their fists up into touchdown position with the beat between claps.

Clap, clap, clap, clap.

"Let's go, Falcons!"

Clap, clap, clap, clap.

"Let's go, Falcons!"

Clap, clap, clap, clap.

"Last time," called Natasha, which was their signal to wrap it up.

"Let's go, Falcons!"

They ended in touchdown and this time held it while both coaches applauded and grinned.

"That's my squad!" declared Coach Casey as Sophia and the rest of the squad snapped back into clean. "Okay! Now, it's our turn to give our attention to Coach Saunders. At the start of every season, I like to have the coach of the team we're supporting meet us and let us know how they like to be cheered. Coach?" She stepped back to let him stride forward. "Take it away. We're all ears."

"Thanks, Casey." He folded his arms across his chest and breathed in deeply through his nose. He waited a second before letting the air out as he looked out over the crowd. "First of all, some basics," he said in a deep, serious voice. It was a voice that said, *Pay attention! I'm only going over this one time*. "They're simple, but important," he went on. "Number one." He held up a thumb. "When our team has the ball, we're on offense. We're on defense when the other team's running the ball. There have been times," he said, "when cheerleaders started chanting 'defense' when we were trying to score. And, well . . ." He sighed regretfully. "Let's just say that's not very helpful."

Coach Casey spoke up. "It's embarrassing."

Coach Saunders nodded. "If you're not familiar with the game of football, I suggest you make yourself familiar pretty quick. You won't be sorry, either. Trust me. It's a beautiful, beautiful game."

Could he sound more like my dad? thought Sophia. She glanced at Kendall, who was making the tiniest *you have got to be kidding* face. Sophia grinned, agreeing completely. Still, she was happy in the knowledge that she and football were *quite* familiar with each other, thanks to her dad.

The coach cleared his throat and continued. "When do I *like* to hear cheers from the sidelines?" He uncurled a finger to count each one off. "During time-outs. Between plays. When defensive and offensive teams switch. During halftime. And, of course" — he moved to his other hand — "I want you to knock yourselves out every time we get a touchdown."

He closed his hands back into fists and folded his arms across his chest again. "It's also important when *not* to cheer — which is during the actual plays. That's when the crowd needs to be watching the game. And *you* should be watching, too, in case the play comes your way, so a player or players don't run you over like a train." He snorted. "We've seen *that* happen before, Coach Casey, haven't we?"

Coach Casey winced and nodded.

At the front, Natasha turned a guilty shade of pink.

"And, well, finally, I know I don't have to say this . . . but I'm going to anyway. Please. Do not cheer when the *other* team scores. That can really get our players — not to mention me — upset." The coach narrowed his eyes and let the image sink in before he grinned.

"And other than that, all I really want to say is thank you. As my son, who's a cheerleader in college, says, 'Without cheerleaders, it's just a game.' Am I right?"

"You bet! That's why we're here!" said Coach Casey, stepping up to shake his hand. "Thanks, Coach!" She clapped, and the rest of the squad immediately joined in.

"I better get back to *my* team now," Coach Saunders said, wagging his thumb toward the double doors that led outside to the field. "We've got a lot to do to get ready for Friday's game."

"Understood." Coach Casey nodded. "I was just thinking the same thing. Oh, but one more thing. Real quick. Spirit posters. If we could get some done and up this week, Coach, how would you like that?"

"If you could get some done and up, I'd cheer for *you* guys," Coach Saunders said.

"All right, then. Consider it done! We'll talk about that later, girls, after practice. Right now, let's start stretching and warming up. Natasha, Ella, you know what to do. . . ."

The captains jumped forward. "Jumping jacks! Ready!" they yelled. "Four, three, two, *go*!"

The squad made it through a series of cheers and the whole half-time dance before Coach Casey let them take a break. "You guys look great! I'm feeling really good about Friday! It's exciting, isn't it?"

Sophia gulped down some not-so-cold water from her bottle, too

thirsty to yell back, "Yes!" She was also realizing for the first time, with a twinge, what *Friday* actually meant. The hours of cheering and dancing they'd been putting in hadn't been just for fun. In only a few days, they were going to have to take everything they'd learned and do it in front of *everyone*.

This was going to be almost as scary as tryouts, she thought, if her sudden butterflies were any gauge. Though at least she was already on the team and didn't have to worry about making the cut this time. Of course, if she messed up really badly, she could lose her place. . . . After all, they had a perfectly good alternate, Mia, waiting in the wings.

"And while I'm thinking of it, before we get to talking about spirit signs — and, oh, that other thing, too . . ." Coach Casey winked. "I want to make sure you guys are thinking about how you want to introduce yourselves to the fans at halftime during Friday's game."

Introduce themselves? Sophia turned to Kendall and then to Sadie. They both shrugged along with her.

Coach Casey explained that it was a tradition for the announcer to introduce all the cheerleaders by name at the season's first game, and for the girls to each "make an entrance" onto the field. "You can do whatever you want — tumble, run," she said. "Whatever you're comfortable with is great. But I challenge you to push yourselves to do something special, and really show off what you've got."

What I've got? thought Sophia. A pretty good cartwheel. But that was about it. Kendall had been trying to teach her some other tumbling skills, but they definitely weren't audience-ready yet.

Coach Casey went on to talk about the spirit signs next, and how the girls should make them and what they should say. "'Go, Falcons! Beat Coolidge!' Spirit sayings like that. Plus the time and the date. 'Friday, four o'clock! Come cheer for your team!' You can bring them to me in the library Thursday morning," the coach told them. "Tomorrow, even, if you can. I'll keep them safe and sound till practice on Thursday, when we can put them up around the school. Any questions?" She waited. "Good," she said when none were asked. "Again, great practice. Captains, well done."

"Wait. . . ." Ella raised her hand slowly.

"Oh, so there are questions." Coach Casey grinned. "Okay. Shoot."

"Didn't you say there was something else — some other *thing* for us you had?"

"Oh, that's right. So I did . . ." said Coach Casey. She pulled her whistle back and forth across her chest. "Follow me to the athletic office!" she commanded, lifting her hand above her head.

Sophia could see several large cardboard boxes waiting when the coach opened the door. At once she knew what was in them, and she could tell the other girls did, too.

"Uniforms!" exclaimed Natasha.

Coach Casey slipped in and called the squad members' names, one by one.

It seemed to take forever for Sophia's to come, but finally it did.

"Here you go!" Coach Casey handed her a folded stack with a blue-and-white bow perched on top — *like a cherry on an ice cream sundae,* Sophia thought.

"Thanks, Coach! Thanks so much!" Sophia said, squeezing the bundle tightly to her chest.

"You're very welcome! Wear it well! It should all fit, but just to be sure, you should try it on tonight. You'd hate to get dressed for school on Friday and find something wrong with it then."

Sophia nodded.

"Okay . . . Sadie!" Coach Casey lifted the next uniform out of a box.

"Here I am!" said Sadie as she burst through the door of the office and Sophia eased herself out.

Back in the gym, the girls who had their uniforms were holding the crisp new shells up to their chests. The sleeveless tops were blue, with white striped trim along the bottom and a white band across the front. Inside that was written FALCONS in big blue letters, all outlined in black.

Kendall modeled hers, along with the skirt, which was blue, too, with the same striped trim. "How do I look?" she asked Sophia.

"Amazing," Sophia said.

"I can't wait to wear it on Friday," said Kendall.

"They should let us wear these every day," Madison declared. "And you can wear yours, too, right?" She eyed Mia, who was slipping her shell over her head.

Mia tugged it down and smiled, contented. "Oh, yes. The coach said I should. After all, you never know when you'll get called up."

"Hey, what's wrong, Sophia?" Kendall had stopped to stare at Sophia.

"Are you missing something?" Madison asked.

Sophia shook her head and tried to bring her smile back.

"Really, I'm not hoping you get sick or anything!" Mia defended herself.

"No, I know," said Sophia. That wasn't it at all.She was just thinking about Friday and wearing her uniform, and how weird she was sure it would be. She didn't have to worry about surprising Gwen, she knew. That was nice to know. But what were all her other old friends going to think when they saw her?

CHAPTER 9

"Bye, Mom."

The next morning, Sophia let her mom kiss her cheek as they stood in the shady parking lot. The sun was starting to heat up the schoolyard, and the birds were already quieting down. A yellow bus groaned to a stop in the circular driveway and let its riders out.

Sophia still hadn't asked her mom about the guy she'd seen her eating lunch with the day before. For one thing, Sophia had been busy after practice, between listing her classes and her teachers and showing her mom her uniform. The whole thing fit perfectly, but the skirt felt *so* short. The blue spandex briefs that went underneath weren't there just for fun, Sophia thought.

And then she'd had the spirit poster, which was in her hands right now, to work on. That had taken a couple of hours, but it had turned out very well. Sophia had known she had until Thursday, but once she started, she just couldn't stop.

She hadn't given up on asking about the mysterious Mr. Judd, but the more time passed, the more reluctant she was to bring him up. Besides, if her mom had been having lunch with a female teacher, Sophia wouldn't have given it a second thought. Why make a big deal, she decided, about something that surely wasn't one?

But then again . . . Mr. Judd wasn't a woman. And even if he hadn't officially asked Sophia's mom out on a date yet, who was to say he never would? From chess, Sophia had learned that preventing an opponent's development was sometimes as important as furthering one's own. Maybe it wouldn't hurt to do some Mr. Judd prevention.

Her mom headed toward the school and waved, saying, "See you later!"

"Okay, yeah. Have a good day. . . . Hey, Mom?"

Her mom stopped. "Yes?" She smiled, waiting.

"Um . . . I was just wondering . . . um, well . . . what are you doing today for lunch?"

"Lunch?" Her mom shrugged one shoulder, readjusting her tote bag. "Well, you know, I brought it." She patted the place where the canvas bulged. "And if it's nice like it is now, I'll probably go outside, I think."

"Alone?" Sophia said. "Or with someone else?"

"Um . . . well . . . if someone's free, it's always nice to eat with friends. Why?" she asked, brightening suddenly. "Do you want to eat with me?"

"No, no." Sophia shook her head quickly. "No, I was actually thinking about Coach Casey — I mean Ms. Kent — I mean . . . You know who I mean. Our coach-slash-librarian. She's really so cool, Mom. You should eat with her — and talk about books, don't you think?"

"Sure, I like Casey Kent. That's a good idea," said her mom.

"Great!" said Sophia. "Then I'll ask her for you when I drop my poster off!"

Her mom looked surprised by her enthusiasm, but not at all upset. "Well, tell her to meet us out on the bleachers, if she's not doing anything else."

Us. The word stuck out to Sophia like those cheer bloomers when she twirled in her uniform. She pictured her mom and Mr. Judd, then added Coach Casey and grinned. Now she just had to find a way to make *us* mean her mom and dad again. . . .

As soon as her mom was through the entrance, Sophia headed in, as well. The library was just past the office, through doors framed on all three sides by glass. Inside, the air had that same quiet, booky feel and smell that every library seemed to have.

Sophia didn't see Coach Casey at first, but then she realized why. The coach was wearing a dress and dangly earrings instead of a whistle and stretchy F.M.S. shorts.

"Hi, Sophia! What do you have there?" the coach asked as Sophia walked up, working to hide her surprise.

"Hi. Uh. Good morning. I made a poster . . . Coach. Er, Ms. Kent."

"Oh, let me see it!" Coach Casey reached out eagerly across her wide wooden desk. To the side was a thin plaque that read MS. KENT — LIBRARIAN.

"Oh, this is great. I love it!" Coach Casey exclaimed as she took the sign and held it up. "'Go, Falcons! Beat Coolidge!' You even spelled it right! People *love* to leave out that *d*. I especially love the glitter." She brushed some stray sparkles off her dress. "Very nice touch! And your falcon's so cute, Sophia. I had no idea that we had such an artist on the squad this year!"

"I'm not really an *artist*," Sophia said modestly. She felt herself blushing. "I actually just copied the falcon from the school's website. I didn't draw it myself."

"Still! Look how well it turned out," declared Coach Casey. "I have an idea. Since you've already finished this great poster, any chance you'd be up for designing a breakthrough banner for this Friday's game?"

She raised her eyebrows enthusiastically, but Sophia felt her face go blank.

"What's a breakthrough banner?" Sophia asked slowly.

"Ah!" Carefully, Coach Casey propped Sophia's poster on the counter behind her, against the wall. She rubbed her palms together as she spun back around. "Breakthrough banners! Very simply, they're huge paper signs for the team to run through when they come onto the field." She stretched her arms out. "We don't always have them, but they're nice for big home games like this."

"Oh . . ." Now Sophia had an idea of what she was talking about. She'd seen those kinds of banners in movies and TV shows. "I could do something like that," she said. "I don't have any paper that big, though."

"Not a problem," Coach Casey assured her. "The art room has plenty. And they have a nice big space there where you can work. I believe it's always open during lunch periods, too, so you could do it then," she said. "But let me just call the art teacher and make sure that works for him."

She held up a *wait just one second* finger and reached for the phone at the end of her desk.

"Hi, Chris . . . It's Casey in the library. . . ." She went on to explain what they wanted to do. "Great! Fantastic! My cheerleader will see you there at lunch!"

She hung up. "Oh, wait. Did you bring lunch?" Coach Casey asked Sophia. "Or were you going to buy it here at school?"

"I brought it," Sophia told her. Which suddenly reminded her! "Do you know my mom?"

"Of course I do. Monica. The nurse. She's great," Coach Casey replied.

"I know!" Sophia nodded. "And that's why I was thinking, you guys should have lunch."

The idea landed easily on Coach Casey. "You're so right. We should," she said.

"Great! You can meet her on the bleachers today!" Sophia informed her.

"Oh . . ." The coach's nose wrinkled a little. "Unfortunately, not today. In fact, not this whole week." She pointed her thumb at two carts overflowing with stacks of books. "Too many new acquisitions to sort, I'm afraid."

"Oh . . ." Sophia couldn't hide her disappointment, which the coach seemed to take as empathy.

"I know," said Coach Casey. "The first week back is always really busy, but I'll be all caught up, I know, by next week. Anyway!" she went on cheerily. "Breakthrough banners. Let's get back to those. They don't have to be elaborate or anything. Simple is just fine. But it

is a pretty big job, so if you want to get some of the girls to help you, go right ahead."

That was a nice idea, at least, Sophia thought. And after a second, it gave her one more. She might not be able to choose her mom's lunch date that day, but she could certainly pick her own.

"How about if they're not on the squad? Could I get help from someone then?"

The coach leaned over her desk toward Sophia. Her earrings brushed along her cheeks. "Are they a Fairview Falcon?"

Sophia paused, not sure.

"Are they a *student*?" the coach asked, clarifying herself.

"Oh, yes. Yes, they are," Sophia said.

"Then definitely. It's their team, too! I like that inclusive spirit, Sophia. You are a born cheerleader."

Sophia left the library with a mission — and also, thanks to Coach Casey, a brand-new book by an author she loved. Excited, she hurried to first period and found Kendall and Gwen waiting for her.

"Sophia! Hi!" Kendall smiled and waved. "Gwen was just telling me about third grade and the business you guys tried to start." She giggled and turned to Gwen. "What was it called again?"

"Deuce Sleuths," said Gwen, quite straight-faced.

"Did you get much business?" Kendall laughed.

Sophia looked at Gwen, who finally smiled at this.

"Um, no," said Gwen.

"We did have one case, remember," said Sophia. "But we kind of had to make it up."

"We hid my little brother's bear," Gwen explained. "Then we got him to pay us in Halloween candy to ascertain its location for him."

Kendall giggled some more.

"I wonder if we'd spelled our signs right, if that might have helped," Sophia mused.

"Perhaps," said Gwen. Then she shook her head. "Probably not," she declared.

"They looked good, though, at least," said Sophia. "And speaking of signs!" she went on. "How would you both like to help me make a great big sign at lunch today for the football team to run through at Friday's game?"

Right away, Kendall nodded. "That sounds fun. I'm there."

"It sounds like a cheerleader thing," observed Gwen cautiously. "Are you sure I'm allowed to help?"

"It's not a cheerleader thing, it's a friend thing," said Sophia. "So yes, I'm positive. And it's all set. We can use the art room."

"Really? That's perfect for me, actually," said Gwen. "I have art

before lunch. And the teacher's really nice. I think I'm going to enjoy his class very much. And, of course, I don't mind avoiding the cafeteria. There's just one thing. . . ."

"What?"

"I'm already hungry," said Gwen, "and I didn't bring any lunch."

Sophia held her hands up. "No problem. I'll share. My mom made empanadas and packed way more than I can eat."

"That works for me." Gwen smiled. "I wish I could have one right now, in fact."

"Mmm. Are they good?" asked Kendall. "How many, exactly, do you have?"

"How many of what do you have?" It was Madison, beaming at them as she closed in.

Mia was beside her, smiling just as brightly, wearing the same lace top and ruffled skirt as Madison . . . and the same shoes . . . and the same waterfall braid hairstyle.

"Aw!" They both frowned and slid their bottom lips out. "You guys didn't wear your braids."

"Oh . . . I forgot," said Sophia. She totally had.

"I did, too. Sorry," Kendall said.

M&M heaved sighs of immense disappointment, then broke into smiles again.

"So, what were you guys talking about?" asked Madison.

"Um . . ." Sophia began.

"Empanadas," Gwen said, helping her.

Madison turned to Mia. "What are *those*?" Mia shrugged, and so did Madison. "I'm sure my parents have some somewhere," decided Madison. "So what *else* is going on?"

"We were just talking about making a banner," said Kendall. "For the football players to run through before the game."

"A breakthrough banner! Who thought of that?" exclaimed Madison. "That's such a great idea! When are you making it? And where? We're totally, totally there!"

"Um . . ." Sophia said again. She could tell Gwen and Kendall were both wondering why she couldn't speak. Sophia asked herself the same question and realized she knew why. Because she'd been hoping to have some "quality time" with Gwen, to use her mom's term. And she knew that if Madison and Mia were there, the quality would probably be less than ideal.

Still, what could she do? They were her teammates. She'd just have to figure out something else. "In the art room. At lunch. It was Coach Casey's idea. Do you want to help us?" she asked slowly.

"Of course we do!" said Madison.

Mia nodded. "Totally! Of course!"

"Oh . . . but wait." Madison's smile tightened.

"What is it?" Mia asked.

Madison clicked her tongue. "We *can't*." She sighed. "We could lose our lunch table if too many of us aren't there. Sorry." She looked sadly at Sophia and the others.

"We understand," Gwen said solemnly.

"Next time," said Sophia as she felt relief wash over her. She was used to chess, in which nothing ever happened unless it was planned and executed perfectly. It was nice to know that there were some situations that worked out all by themselves.

CHAPTER 10

Sophia found Kendall in the hall after fourth period and they made their way to the art room. Or they did eventually, after not one but two wrong turns.

"No, *I'm* not a cheerleader," she could hear Gwen proclaiming even before they opened the door. "But my friend is and she asked me to help. Here, let me help you. Do you want to put it over here, Mr. Judd?"

Mr. *Judd.*

Sophia turned the doorknob slowly, then gradually just stopped.

"What are you waiting for?" asked Kendall. "This is the right room, I'm pretty sure."

She was staring at the door, which had been painted to look like it was open and led into an art gallery with famous works along the walls. Above the door was a hand-painted sign in bright rainbow colors.

"'*EARTH* without *ART* is just *EH*,'" read Kendall. "Yeah, I think this is definitely it."

"Sorry," said Sophia. She pushed the door open and took a step in.

"There you are," said Gwen over her shoulder. She was standing in front of a long table, unrolling a wide sheet of paper from a heavy-looking spool.

Across from her was the man who'd eaten lunch with Sophia's mom the day before. Today his plaid shirt was green and his tie was the bow kind instead of long. His sleeves were rolled up, and on one wrist was a shiny silver watch.

"Hello! So *you* must be Ms. Kent's cheerleaders! Welcome. I'm Mr. Judd. Today, I gather, our job is to make a monolithic work of art to be demolished on Friday, huh? I love it. Reminds me of the artist John Baldessari, who liked to set fire to his paintings and keep their ashes in an urn."

Gwen's face broke into a huge smile. Much larger than usual, Sophia thought. She, on the other hand, could feel her own face flattening out as he talked.

"Yes, a breakthrough sign . . ." she managed. "Um, have you made one of those before?"

Mr. Judd smiled at the ceiling. "Have I made them! Oh, yes. More than a few." He patted the roll on the table in front of him. "This is the fourth one of these that I've gone through in just two years. But really, *you* guys make them. I'm just here to make sure you have what you need. Come." He waved Sophia and Kendall forward. "We don't have

that much time. I'll get you some paint so you can dig in and start making art!"

While he turned and moved to get some paint and brushes, Kendall pointed to his back. "Isn't that . . ." she began.

But Sophia stopped her. "Let's just do this," she whispered back.

They joined Gwen at the art table. Of the four art room walls, one was lined with windows, and another was covered with shelves. These were packed with every kind of art material Sophia could have imagined, along with some things, like empty egg cartons and cat-food cans, that she'd never thought of like that before. The third wall had a long counter with a deep sink and a row of cabinets decorated with color wheels, posters, and crazy illustrations paired with slogans like "This is your brain on art!" The fourth and final wall was devoted entirely to artwork by famous artists and students alike.

"Isn't it cool?" Gwen said when she saw Sophia staring. "If you step all the way back, see what it makes?"

Sophia and Kendall both backed up to the opposite wall and looked.

"Omigosh!" said Kendall. "It's a giant face!"

Sure enough, Sophia realized that it was a mosaic, the smaller pictures making up a giant one.

"That's so cool!" Kendall went on. "Did you put that together, Mr. Judd?"

"Yeah." He turned and grinned from across the room. "I try to make a new one every year. Last year, it was a landscape. I think it was my dog the year before."

Gwen waved Sophia and Kendall back to her. "Isn't he great?" she said under her breath.

Kendall nodded and Sophia shrugged. He could have been worse, she guessed.

"So." Gwen looked down at the ocean of blank paper. "What are we doing exactly?" she asked.

Sophia gazed along it, too. "I don't *really* know. . . ." she said. "All I know is our coach said it can be simple. And I guess really big and bold so people can read it from the stands, you know?"

"So . . . should we write 'Fairview Falcons,' do you think?" said Kendall. "Or just 'Fairview.' Or 'Falcons.' Is that enough?"

"We could write 'Falcons Football,'" said Sophia. "Or what about 'Falcons are #1'?"

"Or how about 'Good luck — and try not to get a concussion,'" suggested Gwen.

Kendall smiled at her. "You're funny."

Gwen shrugged. "I'm serious."

Mr. Judd returned to the table with two plastic pails of paint. One held blue and the other one held black. Two paint-spattered smocks dangled from under his chin. He set the paint down and passed the

smocks out, then produced three long brushes from the back pocket of his pants.

"Thanks," Sophia said as she took a brush. She glanced at him quickly, then looked down at her hands. She found herself wanting badly to stare at him, while hoping at the same time he'd disappear.

She wondered if he had any idea who she was. Did he see any resemblance between her and her mom? Other people were always saying how alike they looked, but Sophia didn't see it quite as much. Her mom's hair was so much shorter and wavier. And her eyebrows weren't nearly as thick.

If Mr. Judd did know she was her mom's daughter, he wasn't saying anything. That was a good sign, Sophia told herself. He might make a big deal about it if he really liked her mom. If they were just friends, though, maybe not.

No. On second thought, he'd say *something* either way, she decided. How could he not? And how could he *not* like her mom, really? She was nice and pretty and smart and funny. *Well, sometimes funny,* Sophia thought.

He'd probably fallen madly in love with her mom when he met her, whenever that was. How long had he been teaching there, anyway? she wondered. Had they eaten lunch together the year before, too? Or had he heard that Sophia's mom had gotten divorced over the summer and decided to finally make his move?

Sophia was glad he didn't know who she was, she realized. That gave her the upper hand. As she'd learned from chess, a strategy always worked best when your opponent was focused on something else.

She also liked that he was there with them, and not off stalking her mom somewhere.

Kendall spoke up. "I have an idea. How about 'Let's go, Falcons!' What do you think?"

"I like it. It's simple," said Sophia.

"It makes sense," Gwen agreed. "But hang on, first things first," she said. She held out her hand to Sophia and smiled.

"What?"

"Empanada, please."

"Ah! Coming right up . . ." Sophia unzipped her backpack to pull out the lunch bag her mom had packed. She took out two foil-wrapped half-moons and gave one to each friend.

"Are you sure you have enough?" asked Kendall.

"Oh, yeah." Sophia drew out a third.

"Thanks a lot," said Kendall.

"Yes, thanks so much," Gwen said. "You know, I would have helped you anyway. But I really do like these a lot."

"Mmm, those smell good," said Mr. Judd as the girls unwrapped them. "Are they homemade?" he asked.

"Yes, her mother makes them," Gwen answered. "She's such a good cook. You know, you might know her —"

"Hey, wow, look at the time!" Sophia exclaimed. "We should hurry up and eat!" She motioned for Gwen to finish and jammed what was left of her pastry back into her bag. Then she stood up and reached for the blue paint, gripping her brush in her other hand.

"Ooh, you might want to put that hair back," Mr. Judd said as her hair swept across the tabletop.

Sophia looked down. He was totally right. She re-reached into her bag for a ponytail holder and matter-of-factly tied her hair back.

"And you might want to sketch out the words you want," he said, "before you paint them in."

"He's right," Gwen quickly agreed. "It's good that you're here, Mr. Judd." She smiled adoringly at him.

Sophia sighed. He was right — again. And Gwen was, too, she reminded herself. But did Gwen have to be so . . . gaga about it? It was most unlike her.

"Do you, um, have a —"

"Pencil?" Mr. Judd stepped up and offered Sophia a sharp one. If he was smiling at her, she didn't see it, because she didn't look.

"Thank you," she said, taking it. She started sketching an *L* while he scooped up Kendall's and Gwen's trash and carried it over to the large metal bin.

"So what should I do?" Kendall asked Sophia.

"Do you think you could draw a Falcon?" Sophia asked.

Kendall winced slightly. "I don't know. I don't think it would be very good. . . . How 'bout you, Gwen?"

"Me? You mean draw the mascot? For the whole school to see? I'd rather not."

"Well, I guess we don't have to have one," said Sophia.

"Or," Gwen said, "we could ask Mr. Judd."

The teacher had moved back to the window and was casually peering out. Was he looking for her mother? Sophia tried not to growl.

"Good idea!" she told Gwen. "Oh, Mr. Judd. Can you come here?"

He was more than happy to help. "But I won't draw it for you," he said. "I'll just show you how. There's actually a little trick to making our mascot," he explained. "See?" He began to sketch on a scrap piece of paper. "The beak goes like this. And the eye goes here. A few zig-zags for the feathers. And you're done. Voila! Try it!"

They each did. And he was right. "That's going to look great when you paint it," Mr. Judd said when they'd drawn two huge falcons, one at each end.

"Yes! When we paint it . . . *tomorrow*," Sophia declared.

"Tomorrow?" he asked. "Why not right now?"

Gwen and Kendall seemed surprised, as well.

Sophia nodded emphatically. "Who knows? We might even need Friday. I think we should just plan on meeting here every day at lunch. I mean, look at the time already." The clock showed they had twenty-five minutes left. "We definitely don't want to rush it. Today, let's finish sketching. We still have lettering to do. And . . . hmm . . . I don't know . . . the falcons could maybe be better . . . or bigger. Yes, they're definitely too small. *Tomorrow* we can paint. Then *Friday*, when it's all dry, we can get the rest of the squad to come sign it. What do you think?"

What *she* was thinking, mostly, was how this could keep Mr. Judd in his classroom during lunch for the rest of the week.

It was the strategy of chess masters: cut an opponent's piece off from the action to guarantee a win. And so what if she had to miss lunch every day? Chess had also taught her that sacrifices were impossible to avoid in the end.

"Okay with me," said Kendall. "I like this room. It's nice."

"I know. It is. I'll do it," Gwen said. "Does that work for you, Mr. Judd?"

He looked at them, then at the banner.

"Of course. That's what I'm here for, after all. Who knows? Maybe I'll even get an empanada out of it," he joked.

"And *maybe* . . ." Sophia said, ignoring the comment, "we could come every week. Not us, of course, I mean. The whole squad could rotate, and we could make breakthrough banners for every game." She smiled at Mr. Judd's wide-eyed reaction. "That's why you're here, right? I'll ask Coach Casey what she thinks!"

CHAPTER 11

By Thursday's practice, Sophia was happy to report to Coach Casey that the banner was painted and ready to sign.

"Fantastic!" The coach made an announcement to everyone to be sure to stop by the art room during Friday's lunch. "And three cheers for your teammates Sophia Arcella and Kendall Taylor, who sacrificed their lunch periods this week to make us a breakthrough!"

The three cheers were extremely nice — and got some regretful looks from M&M. After that, the rest of practice went really, really well. The squad's sideline cheers sounded strong, and they had the halftime dance pretty much down. Sophia was even doing it in her dreams, which had to be a good sign, she thought.

The only thing she wasn't feeling great about was her halftime introduction.

Each cheerleader performed her own for the squad individually, and Sophia carefully watched them all. Not everyone was a tumbler,

of course. Most of the girls stuck to cartwheels and round-offs. A few simply charged out, spiriting and hitting arm motions as they ran along. Kendall's tumbling run was by far the most impressive, since she'd been a gymnast for so many years. That was why, even though she was new and a sixth grader, the coach announced she'd be going at the end.

"The crowd loves a grand finale. And that's exactly what that full twisting layout is, Kendall," Coach Casey said.

When it was her turn, Sophia did a line of straight-enough cartwheels. She was dizzy by the time she stopped.

"That was good," Kendall told her. "But why don't you add a walkover? I know you can do them. I taught you how."

"I know. I was thinking about it," said Sophia. "But what if I plant my head in the grass? Or just miss completely and land flat out on my back?"

"Well, like I've told you, if you just remember to make a tight bridge, and not let your legs go too far out, you'll be okay." Effortlessly, Kendall did one the wrong way and then one the right way to show exactly what she meant. "See, the closer your hands are to your feet, the less chance there is that you'll collapse. Or you could do a back walkover, if those are easier. Or do both! Why not?"

"Because it's *tomorrow*," said Sophia.

"So? Who cares? You can practice tonight."

"I have homework. And so do you," Sophia reminded her. Not that the math would take all that much time.

Kendall knew that, too, and her eyes said as much.

"Okay. I'll practice." Sophia gave in. She had to admit it would be nice to really wow her dad.

So she practiced Thursday night in her yard. Again. And again. And again.

"Those look good!" her mom called through the sliding screen door before she waved Sophia in to bed.

Friday, Sophia woke up and had her whole uniform put on before she promptly slipped it off. She realized she had to eat breakfast, and she sure didn't want a big orange juice stain ruining the front.

After she ate, she went back into her room and put the whole thing on again: briefs, skirt, shell, socks, and her still fairly new-looking cheer shoes. The long-sleeved blue bodysuit would have to wait for a cooler afternoon.

They also had their "game-day bow," as the older girls called it, which was actually made of two bows. It was blue and white, and nice and stiff, and attached to a thick rubber band. Sophia tied her hair back with it last and stared into the mirror at herself.

She blinked. She felt like a little kid on Halloween, all dressed up like someone else. But this was really her. Sophia Arcella, sixth grader — and Fairview Middle School cheerleader. She stood up straighter, rolled back her bare shoulders, and gave herself an approving nod.

"Sophia! Ready? We need to go!" her mom called.

"One sec, Mom! I'll be right there!"

She turned to her desk and packed her math book in her backpack, then pulled out her phone. She hit "2" to call her dad and waited for him to pick up.

"Good morning, Soph! What's up?" he said.

"Hi, Dad. I just wanted to remind you about the game at school this afternoon, and to make sure you were still going to come."

"I sure am. Wouldn't miss it. I actually talked with Mom about it yesterday. We're both looking forward to it a lot."

"Really?" Sophia's phone slid up her cheek, pushed by her spreading smile. She wasn't sure what was more exciting: that her dad was looking forward to coming, or that he'd spoken with her mom.

"I was even thinking," he went on, "that we could go out to dinner after the game."

"Oh, I'd like that!" said Sophia. "Hang on and I'll go ask."

"You don't have to. I already did," he said. "Mom said she thought it was a great idea."

"Really?" said Sophia again. That was even more surprising news. Not only had her parents talked . . . they'd made a plan to all go out. She suddenly felt silly for worrying about the art teacher, Mr. Judd. Just like with M&M and the breakthrough banner, things were working out fine all by themselves.

"So think about where you want to go," her dad said.

"Oh, I know!" Sophia was already two moves ahead. "Junior's!" That was the place her parents used to go on "date night" — back in the good old days.

"Sounds good."

"Sophia!" her mom called again. This time she sounded less in the mood to wait.

"Well, I better go, Dad. I love you so much. See you this afternoon!"

"See you then, Soph. Love you, too."

Her bow straight and her laces tight, Sophia left her room and met her mom in the hall.

"Oh, Sophia!" Her mom wove her fingers together as if she were about to say a prayer. "Honey, you look so great! I want to take a picture! Stand right there — and smile for me. Real quick."

"Mom." Sophia groaned while her mom pulled her phone out.

"Don't roll your eyes at me," said her mom. "Smile! Isn't that what cheerleaders do, after all?"

Click.

Her mom checked the picture. "Nice!" she declared, turning the phone around to show Sophia the screen.

Sophia bit her lip, but then grinned. She had to admit it was pretty cute. But honestly, she was a lot more interested in the fact that her mom was dressed up.

"You look nice!" Sophia said, pleased. Her mom had on a dress she'd never seen before, in her dad's favorite color, red. On her feet were sandals with a little bit of a heel. Her mom was taking this dinner thing pretty seriously, Sophia was delighted to realize. If only she'd thought to tell her dad to skip his usual "casual" combo and look for something new. Oh, well. She'd send him a text when she got to the car, she decided. There was still plenty of time for that.

Her mom, meanwhile, put her phone back and self-consciously smoothed her skirt. "Thanks," she told Sophia. "I haven't worn this dress in forever. It's not too dressy, do you think?"

"No way. It's perfect," said Sophia.

"Well, good," said her mom, "'cause I don't have time to change. Let's go." She pushed the door open. "You don't want to be late on this big day!"

School could not go fast enough for Sophia. Every class seemed twice as long as usual. And it wasn't because she couldn't wait for the football game. In fact, she became more nervous the closer it got. And it wasn't because she wanted the whole thing to be over so she could go out to dinner with her dad *and* her mom. No, it was because she felt so unbelievably self-conscious in her brand-new uniform.

Not everybody from her old school knew she was on the squad. Basically, just Gwen and a few other old friends did so far. And even so, it was one thing to say she was a cheerleader, and another to show up looking like one.

Sophia hadn't even walked all the way into the school before she could feel the slack-jawed stares.

"Were we supposed to wear costumes today?" she heard a sixth-grade boy she knew exclaim, slightly panicked, to a friend.

It gave her a flashback, miserably, to Spirit Week the year before at her old school, when she totally forgot that Monday was Crazy Hat Day. Her bare head hadn't gotten any stares. But the pajamas she had mistakenly worn sure did.

Sophia wondered if the boys on the football team felt the same way in their jerseys, which they all wore on game day. She watched a few climb off the bus. They looked pretty comfortable, she had to say.

It was reassuring, at least, to meet other girls from the squad in the hallways and huddle to talk about the game. All the other kids seemed to look less at Sophia, specifically, and more at the squad as one big blue-and-white *thing*.

Kendall hopped up behind her just outside their homeroom.

"So how do you feel in your uniform?" she asked.

"Totally self-conscious," Sophia admitted. "It's like, 'Hey, everyone! Look at me!' You know?"

"Yeah, I do." Kendall laughed and tugged at the edges of her skirt. "But we'll get used to it, I think. And at least they're comfortable," she said. "That's another thing I like about cheering better than gymnastics."

"What do you mean?" Sophia asked.

"Those gymnastics unitards are so *tight*," Kendall explained. "And the wedgies!" She cringed.

"Oh, boy . . ." A solemn voice interrupted them.

Sophia and Kendall turned to see Gwen striding down the hall. Her eyes scrolled, unblinking, from their ponytails all the way down to their socks.

"Now it's really sinking in that you're doing this," Gwen said as she reached them and shook her head. "I was trying to imagine what you would look like."

"And what do you think?" Sophia asked. She tried to sound as if she were teasing, but her nervousness was there.

"You look . . . like cheerleaders," Gwen declared.

"We'll take that as a compliment," said Kendall.

"Yes. Please do," Gwen agreed just as Hannah and Josh, their friends from their old school, walked up to them.

"Hey, Gwen." Hannah waved. "Wait. *Sophia?*" She stopped so suddenly that Josh nearly tripped. "You're a *cheerleader*?" she gasped, squeezing her cheeks between her hands.

"I told you she was," said Gwen.

Josh stared at Sophia, too, and he and Hannah traded looks.

"I know . . . but we thought you were joking," Josh confessed, wrinkling his forehead.

"And *why* would I joke about *that*?" Gwen asked. She crossed her arms and waited while Josh and Hannah shrugged.

Sophia stood there as they did, wishing she could change her clothes. She was still proud to be a Falcons cheerleader. But if she could have been an *invisible* cheerleader, that would have worked for her.

She waited for Josh to make some "joke" about the whole thing, since he never missed a chance. Then Hannah would laugh. Then Sophia would try to explain. . . .

"That's cool. Good for you," said Hannah.

Huh? Sophia did a double-take.

"We know a cheerleader! Awesome!" Josh said. Then he pointed to Kendall. "Hang on. You're Kendall, right?"

Sophia watched her smile and nod.

"Cool," said Josh. "We know *two* cheerleaders now."

Sophia gulped down her surprise, along with the explanations she didn't need to give. She was trying to think of something else to say when Hannah started to tug on Josh's hand.

"We need to get to homeroom," said Hannah. "We can't be late. Again."

"Right. Later." Josh waved to the girls. "Oh, hey!" He stopped and pointed to his head. "If you guys need a mascot, tell me. Here's your Fairview Falcon, right here!"

By lunchtime, at least twenty kids had said straight out to Sophia, "You're a cheerleader? *How?*" Another ten had asked the same question but inserted "Why?" in place of "How?" But while some looked a little skeptical, no one gave her a hard time. Most, in fact, acted more impressed by the news than surprised. That made it a lot easier for Sophia to remember to remind them to come to the game if they could. After all, as the coach had told them: "There's no 'I' in 'cheerleading,' ladies. It's all for one and one for all. On game day, and every day,

promoting the game and spirit is job number one! Get out there and don't forget: It's all about school — and squad!"

Sophia had listened to Coach Casey and nodded and thought she understood. But she hadn't really known what it meant, she realized, until she put on the uniform.

It sank in even more at lunch, in the art room, when the whole squad came together to sign the breakthrough banner. Coach Casey even stopped in. She was still dressed in a librarian sundress, but it was blue with white trim.

"Chris, this turned out wonderfully. Thanks for helping!" she told Mr. Judd.

"Oh, I didn't do anything," he said. "I just supplied the paper and the paint. It was all your cheerleaders. As usual." He flashed a modest grin.

Coach Casey smiled proudly. Natasha and Ella both declared the breakthrough banner "definitely one of the best!"

"Who did the falcon?" asked Madison as she took a Sharpie and looked for a place to sign her autograph. She homed in on an open space right next to the beak and filled basically every inch of it.

"Actually, Gwen did," said Sophia. "She's been helping us all week." She turned to Gwen, who'd been there the whole time but had been hanging back by the sink. The rest of the squad had hardly

noticed her in all the bustle to sign the banner. Gwen was watching them like a scientist observing cells in a petri dish.

Sophia smiled, and Gwen smiled back, but the squad had moved on to other things. The seventh and eighth graders had classes to get to, and Coach Casey had to return to her desk.

Madison, meanwhile, urged the sixth graders to hurry and finish signing their names around hers, in whatever space was left. "We need to get to the cafeteria, people. ASAP. My sister says game day lunch is a *huge* spirit opportunity!"

After Sophia signed her name, she eased over to Gwen. Mr. Judd was leaning against the counter, just a few feet away. He had an apple in his hand and was using his tie to polish it.

"Well, that was a big success," he said before taking a noisy bite.

Sophia thought about her mom and dad and how keeping Mr. Judd busy at lunch just might have helped her cause. "Yes, very successful," she said with a nod that she hoped wasn't too smug.

"Are we ready? Let's go!" Madison was saying. "Sophia!" She waved from the door for her to come.

"Go ahead," Sophia told her. "I'm going to help put away the banner first."

She stayed back with Gwen, and together they rolled it up.

"So who are you going to the game with?" asked Sophia.

"The game?" Gwen's eyebrows slid together. "*I'm* not going to go."

Not go? "What do you mean? You have to," Sophia croaked.

"But it's *football*," argued Gwen. "I'd rather watch them *mow* the field. Besides" — she nodded to the windows behind them — "it's supposed to rain. Low pressure moving in."

"It is?"

"Well, sure," said Gwen. "Didn't you know?"

Sophia shook her head. No, she hadn't known. She'd never even thought to check. She looked at the big roll of paper on the table in front of them and sighed, imagining it sopping wet.

"Oh, who believes the weatherman, anyway?" Sophia frowned. "And there's more to watch than football, you know." She ran her finger across the big FALCON on her chest and waited for Gwen to get her point.

But instead, Mr. Judd spoke up.

"I'll say!" he agreed.

Huh? Sophia's head spun around. She'd almost forgotten he was there.

"I can't wait to see you guys out there cheering," he went on.

"You're not coming, are you?" Sophia exclaimed.

"Well, I have to see your breakthrough in action," he replied, as if there were some law that said he had to attend.

"Oh, no, you don't!" said Sophia quickly. "I mean, don't feel like you have to . . . especially if it's going to rain." She didn't realize how crazy she probably sounded until she looked at Gwen.

"So you agree," said Gwen, "if you were a spectator and it was going to rain, you wouldn't go?"

Sophia started to answer but stopped and tried not to look at Mr. Judd. "I think . . ." She sighed. "Oh, I don't know."

CHAPTER 12

"Okay! It's showtime, girls!"

Coach Casey stepped up and clapped next to Natasha and Ella, who'd been leading stretches in the gym. She'd changed from her dress into shorts and a Falcons T-shirt, her usual coaching gear.

Her words made Sophia's heart knot in a way it hadn't since try-out day. She looked at Kendall and could tell instantly that she was feeling the same way.

"Everybody up!" The coach waved her arms up and down, and the squad popped from their mats to their feet. "Before we go out there and start cheering our football team, we should do a quick cheer for *ourselves*, I think!"

"We Got Spirit?" asked Natasha.

"Perfect!" Coach Casey replied.

The captains hopped to clean, and Sophia and the others quickly took their places in line.

"We Got Spirit! Ready!" called Natasha and Ella.

Sophia took a deep breath and started to clap.

"We got spirit!

Yeah! Yeah!

We got spirit!

Yeah! Yeah!

We got what? What? What? What?

A what-what-what-what-what-what-what?

We got SPIRIT!"

After two rounds, Ella called, "Last time!"

Sophia lunged forward at the end.

"Who's got spirit?" called Coach Casey. She put her hand to her ear.

"WE DO!" yelled all twenty girls so loudly it gave Sophia goose bumps.

Coach Casey nodded. She seemed satisfied. "Then let's get out there and show it! What are we waiting for! Go, go, *go*!"

The captains carried the banner, which had been carefully taped to two long, skinny poles. A few slits had been cut in the middle at Coach Casey's suggestion.

"There's nothing worse than a breakthrough you can't break through," the coach had said. "So this is a little trick. Those football players aren't always as strong as they like to think they are, you know."

The girls filed out of the gym behind Coach Casey and followed the path to the field. Their warm-up cheer hadn't exactly calmed Sophia. But it had psyched her up, she realized, to go out and do some more.

She could see both teams, theirs and Coolidge's, in the end zones going through their own pregame drills. She could also see the sky filling with restless-looking clouds. All that was left of the sunny morning was a very distant bluish patch.

"Do you think it's really going to rain?" Sophia asked Kendall.

Kendall looked up. "Gosh, I hope not!"

"What do we do if it does?" asked Sadie, smiling. "Do we go home? Or wait inside till it stops?"

"Wait inside? Are you kidding?" said Madison. "Unless there's thunder, we stay on the field. Rain, snow, *bees*. If the team plays, we cheer."

"Are you sure?" Georgia checked the sky, too.

Madison answered with an ominous nod. "Um, *yeah*. Trust me, I've sat through enough of my sister's games that I know what I'm talking about."

"I guess you *always* need spirit!" chirped Sadie.

"Right." Kendall made a half-nauseous face. "I'm just going to hope it doesn't rain."

They neared the stands and passed behind them, and Sophia could see the benches filling up. The weather sure didn't seem to be

keeping many fans away, she thought. There were a lot more parents than students, though — families of players and cheerleaders.

Kendall pointed as they rounded the bleachers. "Ooh! There's my family!" she exclaimed, waving. "Hey, Madison, aren't those your parents with the pom-poms?" she called.

Madison checked. She didn't even have to say yes. There was no mistaking the McElroys.

Both wore Fairview baseball caps and blue and white . . . everything. They were in the first row, by the railing, clearly waiting for Madison to appear. As soon as they saw her, they jumped up and shook their pom-poms high over their heads. "Maa! Dee! Son!" they chanted . . . over and over again.

Sophia watched them spin around to face the other way and at first wondered why. But then she saw their backs and realized that their T-shirts had a fancy MADISON inside a giant megaphone printed on them.

Sophia wasn't sure if she was jealous of Madison . . . or glad that the McElroys were Madison's parents and not hers.

"Wow, Madison," Ella said. "You're the first cheerleader I've seen who has her *own* squad to cheer for *her*."

The girls who heard her laughed, including Mia, until Madison shot her a look and she stopped. Sophia couldn't tell if Madison liked

the attention or wished her parents would cool it a bit. Her super-charged smile and tightly clenched fists sent two different messages.

Sophia tried to scan the crowd for her own parents but realized she didn't have time. The coach was hurrying them out to the field, and the speakers were crackling to life. The football team gathered under the goalposts while the announcer welcomed the fans to the game. At the same time, Ella and Natasha unrolled the banner along the twenty-yard line to make a long paper gate. Sophia and the rest of the squad formed two straight lines coming from the ends. She looked at the falcon painted on her side and felt a rush of pride. If only Gwen were there to see it . . .

She checked the stands, where she could still see Madison's parents. They were impossible to miss. But from where she was standing, the rest of the crowd was basically just a sea of fans. Then suddenly a jolt shot up her spine as Sophia realized something else: Cheering for them was exactly what she'd been training so hard for since the middle of August.

"You know what to do!" said Coach Casey as she gave the squad a thumbs-up and backed away.

"And now!" the announcer called. "Please welcome to the field! Your Fairview! Falcons! Football! Team!"

"Yaaaayyyyy!"

The players charged easily through the banner. Really, they trampled more than they tore. They ran between the lines of cheerleaders while Sophia clapped and kicked and punched along with all the other girls.

Sophia tried, but she didn't recognize a single player. They all looked the same in their helmets and pads. She didn't recognize the banner now, either. It was just a face-down tattered mess. But making the banner had been worth it, she thought. It had truly gotten the players pumped up. And the crowd was on their feet. The squad had definitely done their job. And they were just getting started!

Before Sophia knew it, the game had begun, and she was on the sidelines waiting for Ella and Natasha to lead them in cheers between plays. She stood, just as they'd practiced, in a line between Kendall and Sadie, with her arms behind her back. A few girls down, Madison reached up to straighten her bow — a no-no that Ella soon stopped.

"But I have to," Madison argued.

"Shhh! No, you don't. And no talking," Natasha warned.

Sophia peered over her shoulder and scanned the stands again. This time she saw them — her mom and her dad — at last. Her mom looked especially pretty. And her dad . . . he looked the same. Baseball cap. Whiskers. When she'd texted him, she should have reminded him to shave. But they were together! They waved. And Sophia waved back. She saw her dad lean over to say something in her mom's ear

and she almost squealed. She hadn't seen them that close in what seemed like years. *Check,* she thought. *And mate!*

Who knew that her joining the squad would end up doing something so great!

"We Say, You Say!"

Sophia heard Natasha and turned and jumped to attention, wanting to make sure she did this right.

"We say 'Fairview,' you say 'Falcons'!" she chanted along with the squad, clapping on every other beat.

"Fairview!" they yelled, fist to shoulder.

"Falcons!" yelled the crowd as Sophia punched her fist up and out.

They did it again and then added more verses, encouraging the crowd to keep yelling back.

"We say 'Spirit,' you say 'Got it'!

"Spirit!"

"Got it!"

"Spirit!"

"Got it!"

"We say 'Number,' you say 'One'!

"Number!"

"One!"

"Number!"

"One!"

They ended, at last, fingers high in the air, then spirited however they liked. Sophia punched and even jumped. She did a spread eagle, which she hoped her dad caught. She looked up to see him whistling with two fingers next to her mom.

"Hey, Sophia!"

She heard her name but couldn't tell where it came from. Her eyes skipped around the crowd. After a second, she spotted Gwen's pale, eyeglass-less face. "Gwen! You came!" Sophia cried. And Gwen wasn't alone. Hannah and Lacy stood next to her, waving, while Josh flapped his arms like a big goofy bird.

When they saw they had her attention, Gwen and Hannah raised some kind of sign.

Sophia squinted to read it.

GO, SOPHIA! it said.

"Sophia!" Ella shook her head sternly. "Pay attention," she warned. "We just scored."

"Push-ups!" Natasha shouted as she pointed to the ground.

Sophia obeyed, along with the other girls, and together they punched out six push-ups, one for each point. The crowd clapped along, then cheered when their team kicked the extra point. And down went the squad again for one more group push-up.

Their team was up. Gwen was there. And her parents were side by side. Sophia couldn't have wished for more. Well, she guessed the sky

could have been clearer, but at least it hadn't rained. In fact, here and there she could see flecks of blue the same color as Gwen's eyes.

Plus, so far, she hadn't messed up.

And the crowd seemed to like their cheers.

Sophia was starting to forget why she'd been so nervous before they came out to the field.

And then she heard a loud, long whistle.

FWWWEEEEEE!

"Halftime! Get ready!" Coach Casey yelled.

Oh, right, Sophia thought.

The game wasn't over yet.

CHAPTER 13

"And now! Please welcome to the field! Your Fairview! Falcons! Cheerleaders for this year! Captains! Ella Kleinfeld! . . ."

Sophia listened as the announcer introduced each squad member by name. One by one, they ran or tumbled to the middle of the field. On their feet, the crowd watched and cheered for every one of them.

Sophia was nervous before they started, but as soon as they did, she felt something else. Impatience. She couldn't wait to hear her name called so she could get it over with.

Finally, it was her turn.

"Sophia Arcella!"

She took a giant breath and willed herself forward. She could hear her dad's whistle through the applause. Before she could think, she'd done a cartwheel, and then another, and another, and another, and then paused. She inhaled again, even more deeply, shifted her shoulders, and laid her hands on the grass. She kicked her legs up . . . and over her head . . . one at a time and walked them around. As soon as

they came down, she pulled herself out of a back bridge, stood up, and joined the line.

The *fweeeweeeweee!* of another of her dad's whistles made her smile and heave a sigh.

"Nice walkover," said Sadie.

"Thanks," Sophia panted. "I'm just glad I didn't wipe out!"

Georgia went next, then Madison, then Kendall, whose tuck got the fans out of their seats.

"Whoa!" declared the announcer. "What do they feed these cheerleaders, anyway?"

All together, the squad took their places in clean position, and Natasha called, "One, two, three!"

"Yeah!" Sophia shouted as they all squatted down with their heads against their knees.

They waited like that for a second . . . which felt like an hour . . . until the music began at last.

As the song blasted out of the speakers, the girls sprang to their feet. All Sophia thought about for the next two minutes was making sure she hit each move. In her head, she counted the steps out, one through four, then five through eight. She was careful when the jump came not to skip any part of the windup so she wouldn't land before everyone else. She reminded herself to point her toes, and lock her elbows, and millions of other things they'd learned.

By the time the music stopped and they jogged back to the sidelines, sweat was trickling down every girl's neck. Coach Casey didn't seem to mind, though, as she wrapped them each in a quick hug.

"Great job!" she told them all. "Kendall, you really stole the show."

When she got to Sophia, she gave her shoulders an extra, *good job* squeeze. "Nice walkover, Miss Arcella! I have to say, you surprised me!"

She moved on, leaving Sophia glowing. That was at least how it felt to her. Sophia was actually surprised to look up and see that the clouds had gotten thicker. She could have sworn she felt the sun.

Parents were gathered all along the bleacher railing to tell their daughters how well they'd done. She spotted her dad and dashed over and hopped on her toes to give him a hug.

"So I was wrong. This *is* a sport," he told her. "You guys are really working hard."

"See! I told you," Sophia said. "Thanks for coming. Hey, where's Mom?"

"Oh, she's up in the stands," her dad said, pointing.

Sophia turned to look up and wave.

And that was when she saw her mom standing there, smiling . . . next to someone else.

Someone in khakis and a plaid shirt with rolled-up sleeves. And that silly tie.

What was *he* doing there? Sophia wondered. She began to push her dad away. "Go, go, go! You need to get back there." He looked slightly stung. "You could lose your seat," Sophia went on.

"Okay, okay . . . I'll see you after the game, then. We're still on for dinner?" he asked.

"Absolutely!" Sophia said. "And make sure that Mom — and everyone else — knows, please!"

She tried to watch as he climbed the stands, but the McElroys' pom-poms got in the way. And by the time they came down, the referee's whistle was announcing the start of the second half of the game.

The coach and Natasha and Ella called everyone back into line. Sophia took her place, facing the stands, and located her dad at last. He'd returned to her mom, but as she'd feared, they weren't alone now. Mr. Judd was still standing on her mom's other side. The sky instantly seemed to grow darker, as if more clouds had just rolled in. Sophia barely heard Natasha when she called out, "Go Fight Win!"

Right. They were there to cheer. Sophia tried to focus and spread her feet. For a second, she tried to smile, too. But that was a little more challenging.

"One! Two!" began Natasha.

"Three! Four!" the squad chimed in.

"Hey, fans!"

Clap, clap, clap!

"Help us out!"

Clap, clap, clap!

"Make some noise and shout it out!

Falcon fans, yell Go!

Falcon fans, yell Fight!

Falcon fans, yell Win!

Falcon fans, shout it out!

"Go!"

Clap.

"Fight!"

Clap.

"Win!"

Punch.

"Go!" *Clap.* ***"Fight!"*** *Clap.* ***"Win!"*** *Punch.*

"Go!" yelled Sophia. "Fight! Win!" She clapped and punched. "Go!" she shouted again. "Fi —" She suddenly stopped and swallowed the word.

She realized she was the only girl still cheering. Even the crowd had quieted down.

She turned to see Natasha staring at her with an irritated frown.

"I said 'last time' like two times ago. Pay attention!" Natasha said.

Sophia's hands flew to her mouth. "I'm sorry!" she mumbled. "I will!"

By then, the second half had officially started and the players were moving down the field. Sophia was glad to have to turn toward them and not have to face the fans.

Still, she couldn't help checking over her shoulder after a minute, in hopes that Mr. Judd had left.

She looked . . . and sighed.

He was totally still there.

"Look out!" she heard somebody say.

Not until she felt Kendall yank her elbow did she realize it was to her.

A split second later, a grass-stained white blur in a blue helmet landed on his back where she'd just been standing. He lay there for a second with the ball clutched to his chest.

"Was I in?" she heard him say.

FWWEEEEE!

A whistle blew and the ref signaled a Falcons' first down.

"Yes!" The player jumped up to cheers from the stands and charged back across the grass.

"Go, Falcons!" shouted Natasha.

"Do it again!" Ella yelled.

"Go, Chance!" squealed Chandler. "We love you! You're the best!"

While the girls around them showed their spirit, Kendall let go of Sophia's arm.

"You almost became a human breakthrough banner," said Kendall. "What were you looking at?"

Sophia shook her head as an answer. She didn't really want to say.

Besides, Natasha was already telling them to line up for a new chant: "Hurry! We're in scoring range!"

Sophia took her place and decided that it would be much better if, for this one, she looked another way.

So she did . . . off to Gwen, who was still on her bench. It was clear she'd been watching Sophia, too, from the way she cocked her head.

Then, suddenly, Gwen's eyes fell to her open palm . . . then drifted up.

Uh-oh.

Sophia knew why, even before she felt the first raindrop.

CHAPTER 14

It rained for the rest of the half. It never thundered, though. It was just a steady, drizzly, endless mist that made shoes squish and glued ponytails to backs. And to faces, too, if you twirled around too fast.

The good news was the Falcons won, 13–7. Which meant a victory cheer for the squad.

"Victory!" called Natasha, checking, twice, that Sophia was lined up right.

Sophia nodded both times to assure her she was done spacing out.

"Hit it!"

"Hey! Falcons!

Stand up, give your battle cry!

V-I-C-T, O-R-Y!"

The squad repeated the cheer until the teams had shaken hands. Then, all together, they clapped and cheered their Falcons off the field.

Almost instantly, the clouds seemed to break up and the rain disappeared.

"That was a good game! A great game!" Coach Casey told the squad as they gathered around her. "Except for a few . . . distractions." She didn't have to name names.

Sophia chewed her lip. She'd known *that* was coming. "I'm really sorry, Coach," she said.

"It's the first game." Coach Casey sighed forgivingly. "Just don't let it happen again. Okay." She clapped. "I want to have a quick meeting, but first go to your parents. I know they want to congratulate you, too. *Oh!* Mindy! Mark! Hi. You surprised me!" the coach exclaimed, spinning around to catch a faceful of McElroy pom-pom.

Along with the pom-pom, Madison's mom was now carrying a megaphone-size bouquet of roses, which she dropped into Madison's arms. Madison's dad, meanwhile, was holding his phone up and announcing, "Picture time, everyone!"

"Girls! Gather around Madison! Here, Mad, you get in the middle. . . . Perfect!" Mrs. McElroy said. "Now hold the flowers up so we can see them. Coach, you can stand right there. Mark, what do you think? Should *I* be in it?" she asked.

Mr. McElroy lowered his phone deliberately. "Of course, dear! It's a picture!"

"Oh, but I'm such a mess," said Madison's mom.

And she really was, Sophia guessed — if in McElroy-speak *mess* meant perfectly dry and even more perfectly made-up.

"Mom," Madison groaned.

"You look beautiful," Mr. McElroy said.

Sophia, meanwhile, sighed and waited on her knees in the muddy grass where Mrs. McElroy had put her.

When it was finally over, Sophia saw her parents waiting. Just the two of them, she was happy to note. She ran over without even cleaning her knees off and hugged them both.

"Okay! We can go now! I'm *starving*!" she said. She took one of each of their hands in hers. "Can we take one car, do you think? Mom, you could leave yours here. Did Dad tell you which restaurant we picked? I hope the menu hasn't changed, don't you?"

She saw her mom look at her dad kind of funny, as if he hadn't even mentioned their plan. Which was really weird, Sophia thought, because of course he totally had. Maybe he'd wanted to keep Junior's a surprise, though. That was so like her dad!

"Well, I think you're going to like it!" Sophia went on. Still, no one moved. Or spoke. "What's wrong?" She squeezed their hands tighter. "Oh, no. Did Junior's close?"

Her mom shook her head and smiled. But not in an *it's all good* way. "Sophia, sweetie, your dad's taking *you* out to dinner," she said.

"And you, too." Sophia turned to her dad. "That was the plan . . . I thought. . . . Wasn't it?"

Her dad let out one of those sighs that sounded like an old tire

going flat. Right away Sophia knew she didn't want to hear what was coming next.

He went ahead and said it anyway, though, while Sophia stared at the grass, wishing he would save his breath. She noticed Gwen a few feet away, waiting for her, and she signaled *Just a sec.*

"Sophia. We talked about this before," said her dad after a few rounds of clearing his throat. "We're divorced now. And we've been separated for a year. And part of that, unfortunately, means not doing things together — like vacations, or holidays, or going out to eat."

"It's not that we both don't want be with you," her mom said gently.

"But we're not . . . a family like that anymore."

Ouch. Here it came. That lump in her throat she always got when her parents talked this way. It hurt, but the worst thing about it, frankly, was that it meant tears were coming soon. She really didn't want to cry in front of the whole squad.

Her dad put his arm around her shoulder. She didn't want to lean in, but she did.

"Hey, we're going to have a great time together. We always do. But . . . if you want to bring a friend or something, you're welcome to."

She sniffed. "I still don't understand. . . ." she said softly.

"What, honey?" asked her mom.

"Why'd you get dressed up?"

Sophia finally looked at her mother's face and was surprised to see her blush.

"I . . . I . . . well, actually," her mom said, "I made some plans of my own when I heard you two were going out."

Sophia cut her eyes to her dad to see what *he* thought of this news. Not much, it appeared. He checked his watch and rubbed his whiskers with the palm of his hand. If he was jealous, Sophia thought, he was good at hiding it.

"With *whom*?" she asked her mom slowly.

"With some people from here at school."

Some people . . .

"Don't worry, it's none of your teachers." Her mom smiled. "Oh, but you do know one, I just found out."

"Hey, I'm back." Mr. Judd rounded the bleachers as if he'd been called up to get an award. "Just wanted to make sure I got my bag and, you know" — he grinned — "use the facilities before they locked us out of school. I saw you cheering, though," he told Sophia. "You guys did a great job. And boy, was your banner a hit, huh? You all looked great out there. Congrats!"

"Thanks," Sophia muttered.

"And how lucky were we," he went on, "that it didn't rain till the second half?"

Sophia nodded, barely, while her parents cheerfully agreed. What a waste her whole "strategy," or whatever, to get them back together had been. She knew how it felt to lose a chess match, and she didn't feel like that. At all. She felt like someone — some sneaky art teacher — had walked by her game and flipped over her board.

Yet . . . there her parents were — together, but not together — acting like friends. They were smiling, and nodding, and doing all those things that people who were happy did. She'd gotten used to them being *together* together and looking miserable. Were they happier now, she wondered, not because they were with each other, but because they weren't?

"Hey, look!" her mom suddenly said. She pointed up, across the field, behind Sophia's head.

Sophia turned to see.

"Wow! A rainbow!" she heard Madison practically shriek.

And sure enough, there it was, rising from behind the trees. It disappeared about halfway through its arc, but the part that was there was surprisingly colorful and bright.

Just then, Kendall ran up and gave Sophia's free arm a tight, friendly squeeze. Sadie and Georgia and Chandler were behind her, bouncing eagerly.

"Hi, everybody! 'Scuse me! Coach Casey's calling us," Kendall said.

"Oh. Okay. I'll be back in a sec," Sophia told her dad. "Um, so, Mom . . . see you later, I guess."

"Have a good time." Her mom kissed her forehead. "You were just great, amazing out there."

"Come on!" Kendall hooked Sophia's one arm, and Sadie took the other, and they merrily dragged her away.

"Hey, Dad?" Sophia called over her shoulder. "Will you go tell Gwen and all those guys I'm coming so don't leave? And tell them about dinner, okay? We can take them. And I'll see who on the squad is free!"

See how Sophia and Kendall made the squad!

"Hey, girls! Kendall! Libby!" Suddenly, their mom's voice vaulted up the stairs. It sounded different in this box-filled house than it had in their old, cozy home.

"Yeah!" Kendall called back.

"Come down here, will you, girls?"

"Do I have to?" Libby yelled, sitting up. "I'm giving therapy to the cats!"

"Yes," their mom answered. "You do! Don't make me wait!"

Libby sighed and stood up.

"Come on, they'll be fine," Kendall said, draping her arm around Libby's thin back.

Halfway down the stairs, Kendall saw her mom standing just inside the open front door. She was holding a large white envelope and standing next to a wispy-haired blond girl. The girl was shorter than Libby, but still looked about her age. She had pink shorts over a bright yellow bathing suit, and a rosy, freckled face.

"Libby, Kendall, this is Claudia. Guess what?" said their mom. "She lives next door. I just went out to check the mail, and I met her and her mom."

"Hi." The girl smiled, making instant dimples.

"Hi." Libby smiled back.

"My mom's going to turn on the sprinkler. Want to come over?" Claudia asked.

"Uh . . . okay." Libby shrugged.

"Do you have a bathing suit?" Claudia asked.

"To watch the sprinkler?"

"No, to run through it!" Claudia laughed. "That's the whole point. To get wet."

"Oh!" Libby understood suddenly. "Like the fountain in the park! Can I do it, Mom?"

"Of course," their mom said. "Ooh . . ." Then she bit her lip and paused. "The only thing is I'm not quite sure where the bathing suits are packed."

"She can borrow mine," Claudia offered.

"I can borrow hers!" said Libby. "Did you hear that, Mom? All right?"

"All right! Go, then!" their mom said, giving Libby a quick hug. "Have fun, girls. Libby, tell Claudia's mom, Mrs. Berman, thank you, and be good! Okay?"

The girls skipped off, and Kendall's mom turned to her. "You look happy. Find your trophies?" she asked.

"I hope. Libby thinks they're in the basement." Kendall and her mom exchanged a *figures* smile. Then Kendall nodded to the envelope still in her mother's hand. "What'd we get in the mail our first day here?" she asked.

"It's from your new school. Here, open it. I don't know what it could be. Let's hope something good!"

Her new school. *Ugh*. The words flipped a switch in Kendall that made her stomach do the twist. School didn't start for several weeks, but — who knew? — maybe in Fairview they went ahead and sent their class lists out early. How nice it would be to know the names of the kids she'd be going to school with, Kendall thought. Maybe some even lived nearby and were hoping to make new friends — like her. Or better yet, maybe the school had a big end-of-summer, before-school-started, welcome-the-new-kids good-old Midwestern picnic!

Just please don't make it summer reading or homework, she wished.

Kendall pulled a stapled packet out of the envelope and read it together with her mom.

Fairview Middle School Cheerleading Tryouts

Go Fairview Falcons!

Kendall read it again. "They have *cheerleaders* in *middle school*?" she said, surprised.

"Hmm . . ." said her mom. "Things are different here than in New York, I guess, huh? Oh, look, it says they cheer for football and basketball games . . . and other school events. That's kind of cute." She shrugged, peering at Kendall. "Interested?" she asked.

Kendall flipped through the pages of the packet. Cheerleading? She'd sure never considered doing *that* before. She imagined herself in one of those outfits and giggled at the thought. But then again, maybe the idea wasn't so crazy. From the little bit of cheering she'd seen, she thought it did look like a lot of fun. Plus her gymnastics experience, she knew, would be a very good thing. It even said right there in the "each candidate will be scored on" list that tumbling could earn you ten whole points.

"I don't know," she told her mom slowly. "Do you think I'd be any good?"

"I think you'd be good at anything you put your mind to," her mom said automatically.

Kendall rolled her eyes. She wondered if parents had to memorize lines like that at the hospital before they brought their babies home.

"I'm serious, Mom. They score a lot for tumbling, and I can definitely do that. And it says they have clinics to help you with the other stuff all week, Monday through Thursday, then tryouts on Friday afternoon. Oh, wow," she realized as she read, "it starts next *week*!"

That was soon!

But also good.

She'd kind of been dreading the upcoming weeks before school started, with no one to hang out with and nothing to do. She could text and video chat with her friends back in New York, of course, but

it wasn't the same. At all. At the very least, she thought, she could meet some girls her age at the clinics and hopefully make friends. And at the most, she could end up a cheerleader after tryouts — and *really* blow the minds of all her friends back in New York!

"I think I should do it. Can I?" she asked.

"Sure." Her mom shrugged. "I'll call today and sign you up. It'll be a big commitment, you know, when you're just getting used to a new school. But I think you'd be really great, and I bet you could meet a lot of girls."

It took Kendall a second to process the "yes" at the heart of all that, but she hugged her mom as soon as she did. "That's just what I was thinking, Mom! Exactly!" she said.

Beep! Beep! Just then, a silver car pulled into the driveway. It was her dad back from some restaurant with two huge bags full of food.

"Dad!" Kendall took off down the brick walkway before he even opened his door. "Dad, guess what I'm going to try out for!"

For anyone who's ever felt that boys were a different species . . .

Twelve-year-old Kara McAllister has a great idea: The Boy Project! By making charts, graphs, and taking notes on different boys, she's sure to find the right guy for her.

If only it were that easy . . .

"A rollicking ride through middle-school affairs of the heart." —*Booklist*

"Kinard creates a highly credible middle-school universe of popular girls, dorky boys, unpredictable teachers, and volatile loyalties; she hits all the right notes . . ." —*Publishers Weekly*